CONCERNING
THE DUST

CONCERNING
THE DUST

A Novel

Corey Emory

Portobello Road Publishing

This is a work of fiction. All of the characters, incidents, and dialogue, except for incidental references to public figures, schools, institutions, or services, are imaginary and are not intended to refer to any living persons or to disparage any person's, company's, school's, or institution's products or services.

ISBN: 0692993894
ISBN 13: 9780692993897
Library of Congress Control Number: 2017963340
Portobello Road Publishing, Cambria, CA

For Laurel and Portia

Angel, angel, what have I done?
I've faced the quakes, the wind, the fire
I've conquered country, crown, and throne
Why can't I cross this river?

—"The Humbling River," Puscifer

There wasn't a clear, identifiable emotion within me, except for greed and, possibly, total disgust. I had all the characteristics of a human being—flesh, blood, skin, hair—but my depersonalization was so intense, had gone so deep, that the normal ability to feel compassion had been eradicated, the victim of a slow, purposeful erasure. I was simply imitating reality, a rough resemblance of a human being, with only a dim corner of my mind functioning.

—*American Psycho*, Bret Easton Ellis

It is idle to point out to the perverted man the horror of his perversion: while the fierce fit is on, that horror is the very spice of his craving. It is ugliness itself that becomes, in the end, the goal of his lechery; beauty has long since grown too weak a stimulant.

—*That Hideous Strength*, C. S. Lewis

I want to fuck you like an animal
My whole existence is flawed
You get me closer to God

—"Closer," Nine Inch Nails

OVERTURE

"How do you think you got to such a place...not just the nightmares and violent thoughts but all of it?"

Silence.

"The way I lived before I accepted God, or even the idea of God, was...*is*...deeply ingrained...I've had difficulty letting go."

"Difficulty?"

Silence.

"Looking back, certain incantations, certain premises, certain axioms were demonstrated to me...from these axioms followed conclusions that did not answer the questions...I was taught the rules at a young age. But then later, I was told that I was random matter...*chance*...that absolutes in terms of ethics were relative; the implications from this led to a sense of dread." Brief silence. "The inevitability of my dread was frustration, anger...self-pity... then disinterestedness. I became deeply cynical...and desperate for connection."

Silence.

"I see...and how old were you when you first started looking at pornography?"

Silence.

"I don't really remember...sometime after my parents' divorce...I was probably eleven or twelve when I found my father's videos."

"Would you say pornography was a habit of yours?"

Silence.

"I watched pornography, off and on, for many years... yes."

Silence.

"Off and on?"

"In my last year of college, I started dating. The experience was, for me, euphoric...I would go to church with her. For the most part I was indifferent to it. But eventually I became interested in the answers given to questions of value...meaning...absolutes."

Silence.

"I stopped watching porn during that time."

"I see. You sound disappointed?"

"I knew so little...about myself. I mean, I elevated my girlfriend...in my mind, I elevated her...she became my point of reference...an anchor. After college, I accepted a job as a business consultant...the work was interesting and went well for a couple of years, but I became dissatisfied. I ultimately accepted a position as chief fundraiser for a political party."

Silence.

"What was that like for you? Your professional life, I mean."

Silence.

"I suppose you could call it a catalytic experience…the political world can be…disorienting. Ethics, morality, and particular concepts tended to carry a utilitarian function—a means to an end. The ideals themselves were, for the most part, without content. They simply bred emotion…a feeling of uncertainty. What is certain is that my thoughts, especially at particular moments, were principally dissonant…almost schizophrenic, marked by contradictory feelings of apprehension and certainty, hesitation and faith, ambiguity and lucidity. The initial joy of knowing God became an exercise in fleetingness; it became a duty…I mistrusted God."

Silence.

"I see."

1

A girl who says that her name is Colleen calls into the late-night radio talk show and makes a prediction about when the next space alien is going to land on Earth. She sounds young, maybe sixteen or seventeen and as she talks, I start to wonder what she looks like. I try to imagine what she looks like naked.

"The visitation will probably take place in the Arizona desert," she explains to the DJ.

"How confident are you about this?" the DJ asks.

"Um, very," she says. "It's going to happen in December, near an old road that was once used but now is, um, abandoned."

"How did you make this prediction...this discovery that an extraterrestrial is going to land?"

"Um, well, I was born in December, and for the last six weeks, I've been waking up almost every night at 12:29 a.m.—it's a warning that something is going to happen on my birthday, December 29, at 1:00 a.m."

"But why 1:00 a.m.?"

"Um, I'm not sure. I just feel it will happen around that time."

"How do you know it will be in the desert?"

"Well, um, it seems logical. Because I live in the Arizona desert with my mom and stepdad, and, um, this is the perfect place because it's so quiet and nothing ever happens here, and when I told my mom about it, she was like, 'Spectacular, Colleen, spectacular.' She kept like saying it over and over. Um, I don't think she could...um, like, handle it."

"I see...I'm curious...why did you use the word 'warning'?"

"What?"

"Warning...you said the time on your clock was a warning...are we in danger? Will this be a visitation of hostility?"

"Well, um, yes, in a way. I think they are going to tell us things, um, information about who we are and stuff like that...they are going to warn us, um, warn us...but I don't think anybody is really going to listen."

"I see. You sound young, Colleen. How old are you?"

"Um, fifteen...but I'm almost sixteen."

Other people call in worried and ask if they should purchase airplane tickets to Arizona. I also consider buying a ticket. I turn the radio off and think about a possible alien prophet, wondering if there are enough emergency supplies in the trunk of my car. I think about Christmas shopping. It's late November. Spectacular.

2

The next morning, gusty winds are blowing in from the west as I drive on Foothill Expressway in Los Altos. Doxylamine succinate mixed with acetaminophen is flowing through my body. The cold-and-flu medicine produces a semi-anesthetizing and seminumbing effect on my brain, slowing my ability to think, to reason, allowing the impending doom that I don't so much see, as feel around me, to ease into my mind and quietly settle. I roll down my window, and the raw wind pours in, rushing over me. I'm meeting the campaign director and speechwriter for California's Republican Party, Mark Schnell, at Starbucks to discuss the day's events and to coordinate upcoming meetings.

I momentarily watch the movement of heavy rain clouds above the Santa Cruz Mountains. A man on the radio is singing quietly. His voice is rhythmic. It pulls me into a sort of trance, reorganizing my thoughts then sending me off in a different direction.

"I can't seem to recognize you anymore," he murmurs.

Mark and I are sitting outside at a patio table. I'm holding a cup of coffee, going through the motions. Mark is telling me about the speech he wrote for our boss, Robert

Wallis, who is running for governor of California. The speech addresses the Santa Clara County Teachers Union, which is made up mostly of Democrats. Mark is saying, "Bear in mind, I actually used phrases like 'benefits package,' 'higher spending budget for teachers,' 'millions for the upcoming fiscal year.' I think I even wrote they 'deserve it for the tough and essential job they carry out.' Christ. *Essential*. Are you listening?" he asks. I nod. He looks back down at a piece of paper in front of him.

"So where were you last night? I called your cell half a dozen times. I was getting worried. Robert is giving this speech today," he pauses, and then almost as an afterthought, "Have you spoken to Maria or David?" He doesn't look up from his paperwork. The question "Where were you last night?" is all that I really focus on. The words cause anxiety to flicker through me. I don't know why. I don't know why the question would cause me anxiety, but it does.

"Evan? Hello?" Mark says. Then, very slowly, "Where. Were. You. Last. Night?" He's looking at me intently now.

"I was talking on the phone to Maria and David." My response is only partially true. I spoke with them, but it was two weeks ago.

Silence.

"And?"

"And...and I was soothing them, encouraging them that this speech was still a good idea." More silence.

He looks back down at something. I sip my coffee.

Maria Rodriguez and David Christianson are both strong liberals and "important" members of the Santa Clara County Teachers Union. It took an amazing amount of reassurance on my part to convince Maria and David that a teachers union meeting with Robert Wallis would help "iron out the wrinkles" in future policymaking between the parties. I told them that "fraternizing" with Republicans, as a lot of the Democratic teachers were hissing, was an overexaggeration. I suggested that a meeting between the two sides would be a good idea, stating that it would be "healthy for Santa Clara County teachers and for Americans all across the United States, because, as everyone knows, 'As California goes, so goes the nation.'" I also told Maria that she was an important player, not only as a woman and a minority but also as a teacher and a Democrat. I told her that she was shaping America. I told David about budget increases for teachers and about smaller classroom sizes. I alluded to safer schools and to giving teachers the tools they need to teach children fruitfully and cost effectively. I encouraged ideas of making a difference among the races. I hinted at universal racial harmony. I told them everything that Robert Wallis was going to tell them from the podium.

"Okay...remind me what we have this week," Mark says, pen ready to take notes.

"Teachers union meeting is today...I'm also meeting with Tom and Brian from NCC, and tomorrow Robert's having dinner with representatives from the California chapter of the National Rifle Association," I say and pause. I think about something. "And that's a fundraising dinner, nine hundred dollars a plate, plus independent donations." I open a file I brought with me and glance over it for a few seconds.

"Let's see," I continue. "I'm working on radio programs…I'm confident we've got airtime with a few of the key syndicates that have massive audiences throughout California—"

"We also want the television networks," Mark says, cutting me off.

"I'm working on those."

"Great. Okay, what about future dinners and lunches?"

"I'm talking with the California Mormon Churches and Tabernacles, GOPAC, the Republican Jewish Coalition, the Republican National Hispanic Association, and the African American Republican Leadership Council. Just as a heads-up, Mark: I recommend speeches on abortion, immigration laws, equal opportunity changes, energy sustainability, we can never press education too much, state budget—"

"Wait," Mark says, holding up a hand. He pauses and then very slowly says, "California Mormon Churches and Tabernacles? Do we really want that kind of…association?"

I'm looking at the clouds behind Mark—threatening clouds—edging further over the valley. I begin to wonder if there is anyone out there who would understand what I mean by the word "escape." A cold wind rushes over us.

I look at the couple sitting a few tables away. Autumn has almost faded completely from the Bay Area. The forecast calls for strong winds and temperatures in the low fifties with strong chances of rain all week. I'm out of painkillers. This is what I'm thinking about when I say, "A lunch with reps from the Mormon church is probably worth over a quarter of a million dollars."

3

Later, it's raining as I drive south on Highway 17. The clouds over the Santa Cruz Mountains somehow seem thicker. Darker. Traffic is choking, as usual, a stop-and-go surge of men, women, and children making their way down a California highway. The cold-and-flu medicine has worn off, and I'm trying not to panic. I struggle to think about something else. I turn the radio on to the sound of a commercial. Another commercial comes on, and then another. My mood shifts as I listen to an ad on how to quit smoking, full of statistical data. I change the station, landing on a discussion about how people use their sexuality to get what they want. The phone lines are open:

"Okay, callers, in the last twenty minutes, we've had six men and ten women call in, claiming that they have used everything from their eyebrows, eye color, and even their feet to get people to buy or to do something for them. Our next caller is Heidi from Miami. Hello, Heidi?" the DJ asks. There is silence and static. I really need a few drinks or some codeine.

"Heidi...are you there?"

"Yeah...I'm here. Can you hear me?"

"Yes—are you on a cell phone?"

"Yeah. I'm on the highway. I'm a first-time caller—I'm a little nervous, but I just love you. I listen to your show almost every day."

"Thanks for calling in—don't be nervous," the DJ says. "Give us the goods, Heidi. How do you use sexuality to get what you want?"

"Well...it was mostly when I was younger and in college."

"Okay," the DJ says. I think I detect what sounds like expectancy in her voice—a need for details.

"Well, first of all, I'm a natural brunette, but when I was younger, I dyed my hair strawberry blond—it was a really good look on me. I even did a little modeling. A lot of guys liked me. I was able to get them to buy me almost anything. Cigarettes, drinks, clothes; I even got one guy to buy my textbooks for two semesters. I think that's okay. Why not, you know? Why not use your beauty? It's powerful in a way. It's control."

"Somebody paid for your school books? How much money are we talking about?" the DJ asks.

"Umm...I don't really remember, maybe five or six hundred dollars—"

"Five or six hundred dollars! Did you ever do anything for all the stuff these guys bought you?" the DJ asks, expectantly.

"Nope. I was playful, and on one occasion, a married sociology professor gave me his number."

"Did you call him?"

"No."

"Now let me ask you, Heidi. Did you appreciate having this control back then?" the DJ asks.

"Oh yeah. I knew. You realize it quickly, you know, when everybody is always telling you how good looking you are. I used my looks to get what I wanted."

Traffic picks up and I change the radio station. A song I like is playing and the music pulls me away from wondering what Heidi's hair looks like; what it would feel like, and if it would have any power over me.

I'm on my way to a meeting in Santa Cruz with the vice presidents of the National Christian Council. The NCC is an elite group of extremely accomplished Christian men and women who help various organizations with financial, spiritual, political, and legal decisions while also offering substantial monetary support. Some of their "clients" include major Christian publishing houses, movie production companies, high-ranking government officials, executives of international and domestic companies, board members of large Midwestern distribution corporations, metropolitan hospitals, and major universities on both coasts. The NCC is interested in supporting Robert Wallis as California's next governor, and today's meeting with them could reap large financial contributions to the campaign, as well as votes.

4

In Santa Cruz I stand in the rain and make a call from a pay phone because I don't know if Tyler has caller ID. And I don't want him to see my cell phone number if he does. During the conversation, he informs me that he is out of town and can't deliver anything to me.

"But I called your home number," I say.

Silence.

"And?" he says.

"And...you picked up the phone."

"No, I didn't," he says slowly, cautiously. I freak out and I can't be sure but I may or may not scream at him and I may or may not threaten him. And after twenty frustrating minutes of negotiations, he tells me to call him back in ten minutes.

"Why ten minutes? I don't have ten minutes. I'm already late as it is," I scream.

"So I can find a friend of mine to bring you something now, man."

Fifteen minutes later, he tells me to go to the "hollow," which is a large multichambered underground cave in the mountains were college kids go to party, buy and sell drugs, and write messages in glow-in-the-dark paint on the ceiling and walls.

When I get there, it's not raining as hard. The area appears abandoned. I look down the cave's entrance. There are steel rungs cemented into the side leading into the darkness, and I'm vaguely aware of the possibility of murder, rape. About fifteen minutes later, a young girl walks up the path. She tells me her name is Lori. She's wearing sandals, jeans, a tie-dyed T-shirt, and, over this, a red button-up shirt that is obviously a man's and way too big for her. Despite that, I'm still able to notice she's skinny and has small breasts. I can't help but wonder if she is one of those people that still believe in the hippie movement.

"Evan?" she asks.

"Yes," I say. I wonder what kind of vehicle she has—if she drives around searching for peace. Peace. An urge grows inside me with this thought. Temptation. Her eyes are dark brown, and her hair is also brown and straight. She senses something and informs me, "I'm not alone man, so no bullshit."

"Hey, it's cool," I say, holding my hands up in mock surrender. She looks around. I fight the urge to start laughing. She's obviously scared, and I can't help but imagine her 'backup' smoking marijuana even as we speak. Whoever it is probably wouldn't hear her scream. I hand her two hundred dollars that in turn buys me fifty Nembutal. I swallow one. Suddenly another young girl walks up the trail. She's barefoot and wearing a long plain dress and a heavy denim jacket. Lori looks pissed. "I told you to wait in the van," she says, glaring.

"I just wanted to make sure you were okay," the young girl, probably early twenties, says calmly. She's holding a mango in her hand. I smile. She smiles back. She has high cheekbones and clean skin. Her eyes are pale blue and her hair is long, wavy, and light brown with blond highlights. Around her throat is a blue velvet choker with a silver peace symbol attached to it. I wonder if she is the one I'm looking for...I wonder if we could escape together. I say "Hi." She hands me the mango. They leave. I look down at the mango in my hand.

5

Tom Edmund, Brian Frisch, and I have been sitting in a conference room at Santa Cruz Christian Church for over an hour. I picked this church as a meeting place to help me with the sell. Fancy was not the right approach here, no restaurants or hotels. The room has been remodeled into a sort of coffee house, and one of the walls is constructed entirely out of glass. From where I'm sitting, I can see the lobby through the glass, which brings me relief for some reason. Escape?

"It's complicated...you understand, Evan?" Tom is saying. He stops talking and looks at me. I nod carefully, solemnly. Tom looks at Brian, then back at me. I cough. I try not to look at the lobby.

"Of course, we exercise our powers of recourse... but...things get involved," he continues. "Like I said earlier, California needs a governor who is not afraid to stand up for healthy family values. I've known Robert for many years, and I truly feel that he is the right man for the job. We recognize his administration's statement of beliefs. We appreciate the programs he wants to push—these are distressing times for the world, Evan. Depression is on the rise, and so are drug use and alcohol abuse. Internet pornography is a multimillion dollar industry and growing every day. Only strong faith can penetrate that kind of darkness."

"Absolutely, Tom," I hear myself say. "I agree completely and, more importantly, so does Robert Wallis. We understand that certain aspects of politics are unavoidable as you pointed out, but Robert is the man to cut through the red tape and initiate programs that work for and benefit California's families. We want the support of the National Christian Council. Robert has made this very clear to me," I stop here for effect. I look at Tom and then at Brian. "We need the support of the NCC," I finish.

Tom looks at Brian; Brian nods, and Tom looks back at me, "We will want to talk with Robert, of course… although we personally support Robert, our clients will want to meet him in person before offering their own financial support to his campaign. Some of our clients—predominantly pastors and local Christian business-men—are going to be attending a conference at Biola University before Christmas. Why don't we get Robert to speak at the conference, and then, afterward, our clients can meet with him for a private lunch. Naturally the NCC will pay Robert for his speaking time," Tom pauses and looks at Brian, who in turn looks at me and says, "Ninety thousand."

"That's very generous," I say, then, "I'll start working on it and give you a call before the end of the week."

"Great," Tom says. We all stand up and I shake both their hands. As we head out, Brian looks around at the building more closely.

"This is a nice-looking church. Do you go here?" he asks me.

"When I can," I say. "I enjoy the Sunday night service. It's geared mostly toward college students, but I still like it." Brian nods his approval, and Tom also seems pleased with this answer.

"Listen, my friend Ross Cobble is currently shooting a film in San Francisco. I'll give him your number. You should visit the set—it could prove beneficial for Robert," Tom says.

"I'd love to."

6

It's still raining when I get home later that night. My cell phone has multiple voicemails on it. I press the speaker button then fix myself some vodka with soda water.

"Evan, call me when you get this message. How did the meeting go?"

"Where are you, Evan? How did the meeting go? Call me."

"*Jesus*, Evan, are you on sabbatical? Where the hell are you? I'm driving up to Sacramento with Robert—I really feel for those stupid public-school teachers—the speech went as well as expected. Bear in mind, they ate all of the food we provided and then accused us of trying to 'poison them with republican rhetoric and tactics.' Dammit, call back...where the hell are you? How did the NCC meeting go?"

I delete the messages and don't call Mark back.

I'm lying in bed listening to the radio. The call-in topic is people who think they're being watched. A caller, who sounds drunk, is explaining to the DJ, "It's like I'm stuck in a movie. I can feel the cameras and people analyzing me...you know...even though I can't see them. But the worst part is I can't seem to get out of the movie, you know. I'm stuck. I can't wake up."

"I see," the DJ says. I sip the drink I'm holding. The show goes to a commercial break, and I turn the radio off. I think about the hippie girl. The mango she gave me is on the counter in the kitchen and this makes me smile, like I have a piece of her here with me. I think about her mouth and face. I think about her skin and throat, and I feel myself get hard. Still lying in bed, I call Brooke, who lives in Menlo Park, a thirty-minute drive from my house in Los Altos. When she answers the phone, I can tell immediately that sex is not going to happen tonight. Even though I'm sure I could push it, I don't want to make the effort.

"You didn't buy, did you?" she asks after a long pause.

"No," I lie and end up telling her I'm really busy, and just wanted to say "Hi." We hang up.

In my bathroom I swallow two painkillers that I took from Brooke's medicine cabinet—an old prescription from a surgery. I watch soft porn on the Internet for an hour and then masturbate. The orgasm is feeble, which irritates me. I get into bed without taking a shower. I listen to the rain and wait for sleep.

7

Three days later, I'm sitting in my car at the intersection of El Camino and Page Mill waiting for the light to turn green. Across the street, on Page Mill, is a Christmas tree lot. A young man and woman are pointing to a Christmas tree. A man is nodding and smiling, and congratulating them. He picks the tree up and begins to carry it away. Someone behind me honks a horn. The light has turned green. I accelerate and turn left onto Page Mill without looking in my rearview mirror.

A heavy gust of wind slams into my car and slows my vehicle's momentum. I look up at the sky—thick clouds overlap each other. Five minutes later, I pull into the parking lot of our campaign headquarters. Robert Wallis has leased an entire three-story office building in west Palo Alto.

Inside is total chaos as usual. Over one hundred people, including some volunteers, are making signs and buttons, answering phone calls, accepting donations, getting coffee, photocopying flyers, and working on computers. I pass by clusters of people laughing and talking loudly. Once inside my office, I shut the door and lock it. There is a stack of phone messages for me on top of my desk, along with files and phone books from different counties. I sit down and try not to sigh. Maps of all of the counties in California cover two walls. Either "friend" or "foe" is written above each map. My phone rings and I pick it up. It's Mark. I look down at the sleeping bag and pillow on the floor.

We end up talking for almost two hours. I inform him that Robert has been invited to speak at a conference at Biola University.

"So," Mark says, just before I'm about to hang up. "Why didn't you call me back the other night?"

Spectacular.

8

ater that night, I'm lying on my bed, looking up at the
ceiling. The winds have picked up and are pounding
against the house and windows. I worry about power out-
ages and try to ignore images of my bedroom walls collapsing on top of me. Crushing me to death. A woman on
the AM radio is reading off the news:

"Five more people died when a man driving a truck
blew himself up on a busy street in Syria today," she says
indifferently. My phone rings.

"Hello?"

"Evan?"

"Yes."

"This is Ross Cobble. Tom Edmund gave me your
number."

"—In national news, two teenage boys from
Connecticut were arrested after one of the boys' parents
called the police—"

"Hey, how's it going?" I ask.

"I'm not calling too late, am I?"

"—Are accused of kidnapping a fellow high school
student and raping her—"

"No, not at all," I say.

"—Murdering her and cutting her body into pieces—"

"Tom said you might be interested in visiting the set."

"—A ritualistic attempt—"

"Yeah, um…"

"—To 'honor' Jack the Ripper—"

"What's good for you?"

"Let's see," I say and pause.

"—Parents called police after—"

"Um, I'm pretty busy," I say.

"—Home video of the crime—"

"How about sometime after Christmas?" I suggest.

"—Police Chief praises parents for coming forward—"

"Okay, great. We should be shooting at the conservatory then. Do you know where that is?"

"—He said, 'This is by far the ugliest crime I've ever seen. I'm deeply saddened.'—"

"Yes, I know the place," I say.

"Okay, I'll give you a call if anything changes."

"—Memorial for the girl is being planned—"

"Sounds good," I say. We hang up.

"—The girl's identity is being withheld—"

9

Mark calls. He's really pleased. He tells me the Biola conference went very well. That, "the donations were phenomenal. It definitely gave us a huge boost for more campaign advertisements." And for me to, "keep up the good work."

10

Sometime later, maybe a week, maybe two, I don't really know, I'm walking with Brooke on University Ave in Los Altos. I'm mildly drunk, and the night sky is clear and surprisingly warm. The street has been blocked off, and hundreds of people are walking around, looking at the display of Christmas lights. We walk by cookie and hot cider stands and a stage where children are performing a skit. Brooke squeezes my hand and points to a house with Christmas ornaments carefully suspended over the front yard by string to look like they're floating. The string is noticeable and the floating effect is partly lost because of this. I look up and down the street at all the different colored lights and smiling faces in the crowd, and try to evoke some internal feeling of harmony or sense of community. I can't seem to do it. This doesn't really disappoint me like I think it should.

"Whatever," I whisper to myself.

"What?" Brooke asks, turning to look at me.

"Nothing...I just remembered a joke I overheard," I say. A lie. She looks back at the hanging ornaments.

"We should go ice skating," she says. I force a smile. In my other hand is a cup of cider and even though I don't like apple cider, I take a sip and tell myself it's good. I tell myself that I'm not giving the apple cider a fair chance. Somewhere behind us, people are arguing.

"What was it?" she asks, smiling, and looks back at me.

"What was what?"

"What was the joke?"

I pretend to think.

"I don't really remember...I only remember the punch line."

I turn around to see who is arguing. A guy in his thirties, pushing a baby stroller, is yelling, "Watch where you're going!" at an older couple.

"Hey, Merry Christmas!" the older man, probably late fifties, shouts back at him.

"Just keep walking, or you won't have a Christmas this year," the younger guy threatens.

"Shut your mouth!" the woman screams.

"Well, what's the punch line?" Brooke asks, oblivious to the conflict. I look at her, then at the ornaments, and try to remember a joke I've never heard.

"You shut your fucking mouth," I hear the younger guy yell back, pissed off. People next to me are giggling and shaking their heads in amazement. I fight off an overwhelming urge to leave Brooke standing there and slip into the shifting crowd, disappearing and never coming back.

"Get this," I say, my voice breaking only slightly. "Are you ready...the punch line...the punch line is: I'm losing my mind."

Christmas music is pouring out of a house down the street, and I start to sing along in my head because that's all I can really do.

Later, at Brooke's apartment, we're lying in her bed, watching television. I'm drinking steadily. My face is numb, and I feel easy because of the alcohol. I think about a scene in a porno I watched two days ago. I think about the hippie girl. I think about calling Tyler, in Santa Cruz, to see if he knows her. I think about extraterrestrials.

"What do you want for Christmas?" Brooke asks me. I look at her. I stare drunkenly at her long dark brown hair. The top stories on the eleven o'clock news are the threat of higher taxes for California, and the discovery of a young woman's body in the Santa Cruz Mountains.

"I don't know," I say. She was found naked. I wonder what position her body was found in. I wonder how bad it smelled. I wonder if any animals got to it.

"Well...what do you think you want?" Brooke asks. I push the dead girl's body out of my mind and begin a new thought: clothes, music, maybe just a trip to Arizona, maybe just a revelation, maybe just a connection with a God I'm not really sure is listening.

"I don't know. What do you want?" I manage to say without slurring.

"Too much," she says laughing. I smile and close my eyes. I'm not sure how long I fall asleep for, but I wake up when I hear Brooke turn the television off. She starts touching my stomach. I leave my eyes closed and think about the porno again because it's more exciting that way.

Sometime during the night, I'm woken up by a violent nightmare. I look around the dark room, confused, not sure where I am, but then I see Brooke, curled up, breathing steadily and everything starts coming back to me in pieces. The time on her alarm clock illuminates the message "2:00 a.m." I don't think I'll be able to fall back asleep, so I end up getting dressed and leaving. In her bathroom I leave a note informing her I couldn't sleep, that I'll call her later.

As I drive out of Menlo Park, I stare into the illuminated windows of apartment buildings and homes, hoping to see something—naked skin, sex, or brutal crime.

Later, in the Los Altos Hills, lying in the middle of the road, caught in the beam of my headlights is a white cloth. I'm staring at it. Mildly transfixed. Questions are crowding into my mind. Beyond the white cloth, the road vanishes into darkness. Danger? I want to step on the accelerator and drive away, but I can't. My muscles won't move, won't obey me. Instead I end up opening my door. Cold air rushes in, and I actually gasp. I slowly get out of my car and cautiously walk up to the cloth. My chest is burning, and I'm suddenly aware that I'm holding my breath. I stand perfectly still, listening. What seems like two minutes pass, and the only sound is the trance-like techno music spilling out of my car. Exhale. I kneel down and look closely at the white material. I'm not sure what it is at first, but something about it feels familiar. I carefully pick it up and turn it around in the air. The cloth is stiff, stuck together, and covered with tiny red hearts. I pull it apart...panties. My mind fills with anticipation. I search the panties for blood or semen—some clue as to how they got here. I feel myself getting aroused. Somewhere in the blackness behind me, something snaps. I spin around, sweat instantly breaking out on my upper lip and forehead. I wait for terror. I wait for death. I wait for a man with an axe to come running toward me. I wait for a wild animal to rush up, bite my fingers off, and tear my throat out. I wait for thirty seconds. Nothing more happens. I shove the panties into my pocket and run back to my car. As I speed away, I look in my rearview mirror. The darkness is red because of my taillights. And blushing, I tell myself there's nobody back there in the darkness running after me. I turn the music up. And as I disappear deeper into the hills, a wave of disappointment—disappointment that I wasn't murdered, disappointment that I wasn't eaten alive—comes over me.

11

The next day, I'm standing in Victoria's Secret, waiting for Brooke to show me something she's "been dying to try on." The store is too busy, and the checkout line is too long. I'm dreading the idea of standing in it. In my hands are bags with items from very expensive stores. I compare my bags to those of the people around me: Macy's, Dick's, and trendy places like Banana Republic, J Crew, and American Apparel. I'm satisfied when I can't spot a single bag from any of the places I've shopped.

"Evan," Brooke says. I turn around. Brooke is sticking her head out of the dressing room. I walk over. She steps back so I can see her. She's wearing a peach-colored thong, peach-colored thigh-highs, and a peach-colored halter top that is tight and thin, and clings to her medium-sized breasts, allowing me to see her nipples.

"Well...what do you think? Do you like it?" she asks, genuinely concerned. I think of an appropriate answer—the right thing to say to her.

"It's nice," I say, but I don't quite pull it off. The needed enthusiasm isn't there. She studies my face for a second.

"What's wrong, Evan?"

"Nothing." Silence. Brooke sighs.

"You're hungry. We've been shopping for almost three hours. Let's get something to eat, maybe a drink," she offers.

"No, I'm not hungry or thirsty."

Silence.

"Evan...what is the problem?"

"Nothing...I already told you...I'd rather shop online... so I don't have to be here...be around all these people. I hate their faces," I say, looking at her ass in the mirror.

Silence.

"Oh...I keep forgetting. You're above it all," she whispers angrily. I roll my eyes.

"Don't be a stupid—" my voice stops. I'm looking at the floor.

"Don't be a stupid what? What, Evan? A stupid bitch?" Silence. I'm trying to think about the store exit. Then I remember a young blond girl—great ass—that I saw earlier.

"No," I say, my voice trailing off because there's some place else I'd rather be, something else I'd rather be talking about.

"A stupid cunt," I finish. I'm looking at her now.

"Don't be a stupid cunt," I repeat. It's hard to tell in the lighting, but I think Brooke turns a little pale and then blushes.

"I'll be in the car," I say, and walk away because apologizing is not an option.

Outside, the sky is dark. The clouds are thick and inviting, and I'm tempted by the impossible desire to vanish into them.

12

Later that night, I'm standing on a large open terrace. Below me, gathered around a well-lit swimming pool, are people in groups of two and three. Some are drinking, some eating, some talking loudly, some laughing. I'm pretty sure I don't know any of them. Heavy winds are blowing in from the south. I watch the blue pool water ripple. I sip my third glass of some fancy Napa wine and look back at a young girl sitting in a lounge chair. The sky above her is intense—dark, cloudy, threatening. She looks fourteen or fifteen. I instantly think about Colleen, standing by her bedroom window, waiting for the extraterrestrial that's supposed to arrive on December 29, eight days from now.

The girl is wearing a fitted black satin tube dress and a dark gray cashmere shawl that buttons in the front. All the buttons are undone except the top one. The shawl is hanging open, revealing most of her chest and throat. She's staring into the pool. Someone laughs. I sip my drink. She has long black hair, naturally feathered. The effect is devastating. Depressing. She's not wearing any shoes.

I finish the glass of wine I'm holding and walk back into the living room to get another refill. The air inside is warm. Smells sweet. Perfume. The living room is spacious—a

California design: large floor-to-ceiling glass windows with views of the pool and the valley below, lots of light wood trim and natural colors. In the center is a glass dining table with candles and bottles of syrah, zinfandel, champagne, eggnog, and punch. Around the beverages are dishes of shrimp, ham, various salads, deviled eggs, pumpkin pudding, cranberry tart, and potato pound cake. The living room is decorated with white Christmas lights and fake snow. In one corner is a medium-sized Christmas tree. Someone's children are giggling and pointing to presents under the tree. The noise level is loud, and I regret having to come inside. I move past a semicircle of people around the dining table and head into the kitchen, where there are more bottles of wine.

The kitchen is large and busy. Brooke is standing near the refrigerator talking with Henry and Sarah DeLuce, who own this house and whom I met when we first arrived. Brooke doesn't see me. I walk over to the soapstone counter and fill my glass with wine. Standing next to me is a guy in a Hawaiian shirt and slacks. He's talking with an older blonde.

"So, did you hear about the earthquake in Southern California?" he's asking her. The woman breathes in sharply and puts her hand out to his.

"Oh, I was at my Santa Barbara house when it struck. It was the most frightening experience. I mean—I never felt anything like that before. My house was a complete mess. Total disaster," she says. He nods drunkenly.

I'm tempted to tell them the earthquake happened over a hundred and fifty miles away from Santa Barbara, but I don't. I walk away. Another woman's voice is explaining, "She reinvented herself. It's absolutely amazing. I really envy her, you know, her ability to do that, to reinvent herself over and over. She never looks her age."

Further down the line, a young man says, "When I first saw her, I was like, 'She's so intimidating,' you know? She had that T-shirt that said, 'Getting off on Mother Nature.' But then I got to know her…"

I keep moving, down the stairs, to the first floor.

"Because I'd say it's gross…it defeats the purpose of being with somebody, right? Why would you participate in that kind of thing?" someone else says.

I slip through the crowd.

"Oh my God, I hate rich people…they spoil their animals—just ruin them."

I walk onto the patio.

"Yeah, I'm heading to New York for Christmas. Everybody reads the *Wall Street Journal* there, even the homeless."

I drift past a cluster of women.

"Something like that…the car was still on fire when they got there. I guess the body was also in the car, but they said the radio was playing 'Hey Jude.' Really sad."

I sit down next to the girl in the lounge chair. She doesn't seem to notice me. Maybe she just doesn't care.

"Hi," I say after a minute. Then, "I'm Evan." I can tell she's disappointed, doesn't want to look away from the pool. She looks at me then smiles politely. Her eyes are clear blue and her mouth is glossy, subtle. I think about kissing her. She studies my face for a second and then looks back at the pool.

"Stephanie," she says quietly, faintly. The satin dress she's wearing clings to her body and has a slit up the side. I look at her exposed calf and thigh. Surprisingly tan.

"So, who are you here with, Stephanie?" I ask. Without looking away from the blue water, she says, "I...live here."

"Oh...um...are you having a good time?"

She slowly shakes her head no, and I think she's about to cry.

"You're not having a good time...why not?" I ask, looking first at the people around the pool, then the terrace, and finally into the pool itself.

"Because," she says, her voice almost imperceptible, "Everything's different in the winter."

Four days until Christmas.

13

I'm standing in Brooke's kitchen. It's Christmas morning. The sky outside is clear, bright pale blue with patches of white clouds. I adjust my tie and watch the clouds drift toward the east.

"Okay, I'm going," Brooke says excitedly. I turn around and walk back toward the living room. Brooke is sitting, Indian style, next to a small Christmas tree decorated with only large crimson ribbons. In her lap is an unopened present from me. We decided to only use French toile gift wrap this year. On the floor, where I was sitting earlier, is a monogrammed bar glass, a birthday present from me two years ago, with Brooke's initials etched on it. I pick up the drink and take a long sip. Brooke unwraps the gift: a red glass pedestal bowl. I study her face to gauge her reaction.

"This is great," she says, smiling. Without looking up at me, she continues, "I'll use it for salads...maybe desserts."

My turn. I open a long box: a white scarf from Burberry. I smile.

"Awesome," I say and sip my drink. We do it all over again.

Later, surrounded by gift wrap and presents, Brooke holds a glass of red wine and nibbles on different chocolates. She's wearing a thin pink camisole top and pink pajama pants. I'm slightly numb from the alcohol and turned on. I move on my hands and knees toward her. She pretends to ignore me. I start kissing her neck. She's stiff, trying not to pull away from me. I know she's not into it, but I keep going anyway. I lift her camisole up and suck on her breasts. I'm fully hard now. I pull her pajama bottoms down to her ankles and, without taking off my clothes, I begin to enter her. She's dry, and I spit into my hand and rub the fluid over myself and try again. I slip into her easily. The orgasm is weak.

Afterward, I'm standing in the kitchen again, readjusting my tie. Brooke is lying on the living room floor, her clothes back on. She's gently touching the area around her vagina, trying to ease the discomfort from me trying to enter her while she was dry.

"Do you really have to go into work?" she asks. I roll my eyes.

"We've already been over this, Brooke," I say, irritated.

"But I made Christmas cookies."

"Sorry," I say, shrugging.

Brooke is looking up at the ceiling.

"I'm thinking about changing my hair...something shorter," she says quietly. I get the impression she's talking to herself. I say "Good-bye" and leave.

14

I will remember my mother during certain times of the year. She worked for a large pharmaceutical company. She was "temporarily" relocated to Boston for three months. She called and said she had to stay a little longer that, "things were a mess," that she would "try to be back soon." Three months turned into four. Then five. After six months it became apparent she wasn't coming back. For Christmas she sent my father divorce papers. I got a new bicycle.

15

Later, in the office, I'm talking on the phone with Mark. Mark is upset.

"If I have to write another speech about energy or education, I swear I'll quit," he informs me. I don't say anything. I don't know what to say. I don't feel like participating. He continues talking without waiting for a response. I scroll through my junk e-mail: "Are you in charge?" "She will beg for more after she gets a piece," "Chick's face looks like a glazed donut," "Life will change forever," "Want—to—get—off?"

I think about Stephanie sitting on the lounge chair, staring into the swimming pool.

"Are you listening, Evan?"

"Make it a New Year's resolution," I propose tiredly.

Silence.

"Make *what* a New Year's resolution, Evan?"

"Not writing any more speeches about energy or education."

16

Three days later, I'm standing in my backyard, looking up at the stars, waiting for information from Arizona. It's ten minutes past 1:00 a.m. in Arizona, and nothing has happened. No one has called in to say if an extraterrestrial has landed. A commercial on the small portable radio I'm holding tells me to start buying great-tasting fast food.

Nine hours later, under the influence of Nembutal, I'm on location at the Conservatory of Flowers in San Francisco's Golden Gate Park. Ross Cobble is explaining to a short, fat man the angle he's "searching" for. Ross is wearing a white T-shirt, blue jeans, and sandals. He's extremely good looking, and this irritates me. The actual "set" is in the Tropical Plants Greenhouse, and it's unbelievably hot. Humid. I sip bottled water and wipe moisture off my forehead. A man and woman, wearing matching robes, are standing in the center of the miniature tropical garden. They're both reviewing scripts and talking quietly to each other. Next to the woman is a fake tree with a mechanical serpent—an emerald tree boa—coiled around one of the branches. Near the boa's head is a cluster of bright red apples. I'm told the apples are real. Mist is being pumped into the

"Garden of Eden." I'm told the mist is manufactured. I sip more water.

"Okay. Let's go again, you guys," Ross says loudly. There is a shuffle on the set as people move out of the way. The man and woman take off their robes. They're both naked except for skin-colored underwear. The man has a full beard, and they both have long dark hair.

"Standby," the assistant director calls. "Roll camera, roll sound."

"Rolling," camera one, two, and three respond.

"Sound rolling," a skinny, young Asian girl says.

"Action," Ross calls. A man, holding a remote control, manipulates a joystick, and the boa's mouth opens. Its tongue flickers. Camera one zooms in on the boa's head. The serpent begins "talking." Off camera, a young man starts reading from a script.

"Did God really say, 'You must not eat from any tree in the garden'?"

The woman looks at the serpent and says, "We may eat fruit from the trees in the garden, but God did say, 'You must not eat fruit from the tree that is in the middle of the garden, and you must not touch it, or you will die.'"

The serpent's mouth opens wide, and the off-camera young man laughs. His voice is sweet, melodious, inno-cent. He says, "You will not surely die. For God knows that when you eat the fruit your eyes will be opened, and you will be like God, knowing good and evil."

Camera two zooms in on the woman's face. She looks at the apples. Camera one concentrates on the apples—dark red, drops of condensation covering them. Glistening. The woman slowly lifts her hand up and takes an apple off the branch. The boa flicks its tongue and the young man whispers, "Yes." The woman brings the plump apple to her lips. Camera one is following her movements now. It zooms in for an extreme close-up of the woman's mouth. She presses the apple's red skin against her lips and pauses before biting into it hesitantly. Her mouth eases away from the apple and her lips are wet with the apple's juice. Camera one zooms out, and the woman holds the apple up to the man's mouth. Camera two zooms in on the man's face. He searches the woman's eyes for a second and then bites the apple. The woman is gripping the tree with one hand, her fingers spread wide. Camera one focuses on her hand and then slowly pans over and focuses on the sweat dripping down her back. The snake is moaning and whispering "Yes" over and over. The man and woman face each other. Camera two closes in. The man is crying. The woman is laughing and starts to run in circles around the tree.

"What's camera three for?" I whisper into Ross's ear.

"It's a high-speed camera, for slow motion...we'll put the part of her running around the tree in slow motion later...for effect," Ross whispers back, without looking at me.

The young man is also laughing now. The man begins eating the rest of the apple ravenously. He chases the woman around the tree and they fall down together, the woman ending up on the bottom. Then he kisses and bites her neck. Camera two moves up in time to capture her face as she scratches his back and sighs with pleasure: her face is distorted in terror and longing. Camera two tightens up. On the woman's lips are tiny bits of apple. The mist swallows them both up.

"Good—cut," Ross yells. There's a momentary pause as people recover and then everybody claps.

Later, outside, the sky is dark. Ross and I are walking past trailers and people loading equipment.

"We'll need some shots of meadows and wildflowers added later...for a 'larger' effect," Ross explains to me. "Maybe some waterfalls, moss-covered rocks...also music—lots of random face shots. After all, this is a significant point in human history," he says. There's a momentary silence.

"Do you know what the shortest verse in the Bible is?" he asks me.

"No."

"Jesus wept."

Silence.

"That's really great," I say. Ross stops walking and looks me in the face. I realize too late that he was searching for something in telling me that, but I'm not sure what. I can sense a faint disappointment in his voice when he says, "Tom said I might be financially beneficial for Robert Wallis...how much do you want?"

17

Five-day forecast: mostly cloudy with a chance of rain early next week.

I'm out of Nembutal.

18

Brooke, her friends Elise and Sarah, and Sarah's boy-friend, Justin, are sitting with me in the cocktail lounge of a massive two-story dance club near Fisherman's Wharf on New Year's Eve. The DJ, whom I can see from where I'm sitting, is playing techno music and dancing in place, his hands in the air. The music is so loud it actually hurts my ears.

"I even made a list. You know what I mean?" Elise is shouting to Brooke, who is nodding and stops long enough to sip her third drink.

"List?" Sarah shouts, looking away from the packed bar.

"Yeah," Elise says, swallowing more of her cosmo-politan. Elise is wearing a sleeveless shirt and in her own words, "a modern fit, cropped skirt."

"What kind of list?" Sarah asks, yelling over a new techno song. I look out at the crowded dance floor. Purple, orange, and red lights flash, then stop, and then wash over the people, all the while keeping tempo with the beat. I'm not looking at Elise, but I'm still able to hear her shout, "You know, list ten reasons why you want a guy in your life." I polish off my third Bombay. Four relatively hot young women pose for a guy holding a camera near the bar.

"You want to dance?" I yell at Justin, who is drunk and looks totally bored. Justin is wearing a plaid shirt and jeans. He looks up at me, but doesn't respond. I look at Sarah to see if she notices her boyfriend's drunk, but she's talking with Brooke and shouting, "Did you see their new house—*beautiful*—and he's only twenty-three." Sarah has blond hair. Real. She's thin, but not skinny. She's wearing a purple elbow-patch sweater and black flare pants. An athletic guy, no shirt on, walks by. His face is painted like a lion, and behind him is a girl in a tight see-through animal print dress. I'm able to see her black thong as she passes. Brooke, who's sitting across from me, notices her then looks at me to see if I'm looking. I'm not.

We've been sitting for almost forty-five minutes, and I'm feeling good but nervous. I want to go out to the dance floor, but no one seems interested. I try to tell Justin about a weird dream I had. I'm explaining, "The guy said 'milk and honey.' I swear." Justin nods, and I guess, from my face, can tell I'm trying to convey something important because he sits up and pretends to listen.

"Milk and honey?" he repeats.

"Yeah. In my dream. The guy next to me. I'm on an airplane, and suddenly the wings fall off. The plane starts nose diving toward the earth...We've lost cabin pressure or something because everybody is floating in the air, and

I turn and look at the guy next to me," I pause here to let everything sink in again.

"I'm going to the bar. Do you want a refill?" Brooke whispers loudly in my ear. I nod yes and look back at Justin, who's now looking at a hot, young girl, probably twenty-one or twenty-two, standing by the bar.

"The guy is trying to tell me something," I continue, even though I don't think Justin's listening to me. "And I can't hear him…because the other passengers are screaming. I try to ask him what he's saying but I'm not sure if I'm really talking and he's smiling and there's something warm running down my leg and I look down and I've pissed my pants and I look at him and I'm crying and he's smiling and he keeps repeating himself over and over and I'm screaming at him, 'I can't hear you. I can't hear you.' And then, just before impact, the noise stops and everything becomes silent. And the guy's voice is the only thing I hear. He's looking at me and saying, 'We're going to a land flowing with milk and honey,' and then I wake up."

A new song comes on. Justin nods without looking at me.

"Very nice. I love milk and honey."

Brooke is still waiting at the bar, and I get up and walk out onto the dance floor. The music pounds against my body as I enter the main dance floor; the crowd instantly consumes me. A girl dancing in front of me, wearing a sleeveless shirt and a high-low hem skirt, has her legs spread, and her body is pulsating to a tidal wave of mesmerizing throbs. She has dark hair, and this reminds me of the girl on the movie set dancing around the tree. I smile and lift my hands into the air. The music stops. All the lights turn blue and everybody holds still. Suddenly a deep beat happens. The lights move. I feel myself slipping away. The beat speeds up; people are cheering, and one thought dissolves into another.

Sometime later, in the men's room, I'm taking ecstasy with a guy I've never met before.

"What does this have to do with me?" is written on the stall behind him. I start laughing.

Back at the table, Sarah and Justin are practically having sex. Brooke is drunk and she's telling me, "Are you my ideal match? It's really hard to say. We need...we need connection, Evan," She stops talking long enough to stare me in the face, but she's having trouble focusing.

"I'm looking for a smart man who knows what he wants and has manners..." she starts again, and then it suddenly occurs to me. As she slurs her words, it becomes clear. I nod my head like I'm listening, but I really just want to laugh in her face because I get it. I understand the punch line, and the realization is this: it's easier...less complicated...for me to just masturbate than to try to get along with this woman. There's a loud countdown, and everybody screams.

"Happy New Year, Brooke," I say, smiling.

Outside the club the night air is warm, especially for San Francisco. A woman is screaming, "Don't you dare call them. It's my life. It's my life." She's hitting a guy in the chest, but he's ignoring her and dialing a cell phone. A crossdresser walks by and checks me out.

19

It was late summer, early fall, and we were living in Gilroy because it was cheaper there. The winds were stronger than my father said he could ever remember. They ripped in from the northwest. He stood by the sliding glass door and watched the maple tree in our backyard bend almost to the point of breaking. I sometimes stood with him and listened to the windows rattle.

At first, just after the divorce, he seemed okay. But then he wouldn't eat or sleep. And later he started sleeping three or four days in a row. He stopped taking care of his body. He didn't shave or shower. At night I would lie in bed and listen to the sounds of porno movies coming from his bedroom through the vents.

Toward the end of summer, there was a rash of child abductions all over the valley. No bodies were found, and the whole thing shook him up. He began waking up two or three times a night just to check on me. When school started, he wouldn't let me take the bus anymore; he drove me to school and picked me up. He stayed up late watching the local news, then the national news. He would drink heavily and take pills his doctor gave him. I would watch his porno movies when he wasn't around.

Sometime later he married a pediatrician, and we moved into a large house in the Los Gatos Hills.

20

In Santa Cruz I buy a hundred dollars' worth of codeine and a hundred dollars' of methaqualone. Afterward, I sit on the beach, dry swallow a codeine pill, and watch the sunset. The clouds are shaded bright pink and red. There are a couple of surfers also watching the sunset.

21

It's raining two days later. I'm nervous. Anxious. I'm standing on the second floor of Barnes and Noble, holding a coffee-table book about World War II. I watch people drive by on the wet street below. As they pass by, I try to look into the cars to catch details that will ground me back to some sense of peace. Brooke is standing in the magazine section, flipping through the latest *InStyle*, and talking to Elise on her cell phone. We've been here for almost an hour, and I'm freaking out because I didn't bring any Quaaludes or codeine and I've been looking at pictures of death almost the whole time and the store is really busy, and I don't feel like being in public...I don't feel a connection to any of the people around me. I turn away from the large glass window and look at Brooke. She's smiling and saying something into the phone. I put the book on the shelf next to me and tell myself I'm not really standing in a bookstore. I tell myself I'm evaporating into nothingness. I tell myself nobody can see me. But it feels like there are people everywhere, and I can't shake images of them spilling out of bookshelves, crawling on the ceiling. I clench my teeth and tell myself it's a lie. I think of songs I like. I think of Stephanie sitting on the lounge chair, watching the pool water ripple, and this calms me down a little. I tell myself she's waiting outside in a car for me. We're going to drive away together, and she's going to help me. She's going to save me.

"Are you okay?" Brooke asks suddenly. I look at her then I realize I'm standing next to her, but I don't remember walking over. I want to scream, but instead I smile weakly. "I'm fine," I say and pick up a men's magazine.

"Are you sure? You look upset."

"No, really, I'm fine," I say. Brooke looks at me for a moment longer then shrugs and continues talking with Elise. On the cover of the magazine I'm holding is a young woman with long dark brown hair. She is wrapped in a large, white towel. No bra. She's sitting on a large staircase with her legs spread open. One of her hands is resting on the wall, and the other is pulling the towel down so you can't see between her legs. She's smiling teasingly. This eases me. I open the magazine and find the pages with the same girl posing in different pictures. A photograph from the hardback flashes through my mind: a cat being burned alive in some alley in some country in Europe. I look at Brooke. She's still talking on the phone and looking through *InStyle*. I look around. I think about the two teenage boys raping their classmate, and I'm completely hard. A surge of nausea explodes inside me, and I hear myself tell Brooke that I have to use the bathroom. I walk toward the men's room still holding the magazine.

The bathroom is bright and reeks of automatic air fresheners and stale piss. There are two urinals and a stall. I lock myself in the stall. I breathe rhythmically and tell myself to relax, to focus on something tangible— something real. Standing up facing the toilet, I study the pictures of the young woman carefully. I pause at a picture of her on hands and knees like a dog. She's wearing a pale green thong and bra, and she's by a swimming pool. Her bra and thong are wet, transparent. I focus on her breasts—tan, perky. Someone walks into the bathroom and urinates, then leaves. I'm holding the magazine with one hand, and with the other I begin to masturbate using just my spit. I orgasm, and my legs buckle from the rush of pleasure. And then everything stops. The images stop playing. My hands are shaking, but the anxiety, the violence…the fear are gone. I leave the magazine in the stall and wash my hands. I look at my face in the mirror.

Brooke buys five or six magazines and pays for them with a gift card she got from her mother for Christmas. As we leave the store, she tells me everybody's going to *The Rocky Horror Picture Show* and asks me if I want to go.

"When is it?" I ask, wondering if anyone—maybe an employee—has found the magazine on the bathroom floor yet.

"This Thursday."

"I don't know...I have to see what's happening—don't forget we're having dinner with Robert and his family sometime this week."

"I won't."

It's still raining outside, and this relieves me for some reason.

22

"So...what's the matter?" Brooke asks me over the phone. I'm lying on the floor in my bedroom, looking up at the ceiling. The room is dark, no lights, and I'm studying the shadows on the ceiling and walls for patterns. I'm trying hard to ignore the feeling that demons are watching me—silently opening and closing their mouths—eager, hungry, waiting. I wipe sweat off my forehead and nose.

"Nothing, I already told you. I just need a shower," I say, drained. There's a kind of frustrated silence. My thoughts are scattered. Unfocused. And this is making it difficult to talk.

"Are you sure...you don't sound...I don't know, you seemed...disturbed today, especially at the bookstore."

I suddenly remember the hippie girl holding the mango out to me. A shot of adrenalin burns through my brain and stomach.

"Evan?"

"Yeah."

"Why aren't you talking?"

"I am."

"No, you're not."

"What do you want me to say?"

"I want you to tell me what's wrong."

I sigh.

"There's really," I stop and think about what I want to say. "No point...to that."

"Why?"

"I don't know why. Nothing is really going to change anyway, I guess. I don't want to talk about this anymore."

Silence.

"Evan, would you just tell me what's wrong? Are—" Brooke's voice stops. I brace myself. "Are you taking drugs, Evan? You promised." Her voice trails off. I think she's crying. I sigh again.

"I've got to go," I say. There is sniffling followed by more silence.

"Where?" Brooke finally asks.

"To take a shower." I hear myself answer, but I'm thinking about the very real possibility of extraterrestrials landing on Earth, the effects of codeine on my liver, and the hippie girl, stripped naked, hands tied above her head. I still have the mango, which is now rotten, in my refrigerator. I think about the panties I found—I washed them and masturbated into them—then threw them away.

"I'll call you after I take a shower," I lie. There is more silence.

"I love you," Brooke says weakly. I say "Good-bye" and hang up.

23

The next day, I'm sitting at my desk, listening to music on my headphones. Mark barges in without knocking. This is nothing new, so I don't say anything. I take my headphones off and wait for the unavoidable.

"Did you read the papers today, Evan?" Mark asks as he slouches into the chair across from me. There is a brief temptation to put my headphones back on.

"No. I don't read the—"

"This state is going to hell in a democratic hand basket. Bear in mind, Evan, bear in mind: I've been saying it for years. I will have no problem handing out a few I-told-you-sos when the rest of California, except for a precious few, finally wake up to this fact."

I'm nodding, "Okay, Mark. You sound upset. What's up?" Mark stares at me incredulously.

"Jesus Christ, *Evan*. Are you becoming my wife now? What do you mean, 'What's up'? If the demo-faggots stay in the governor's office, we'll all be swimming in illegal immigrants. That's what's up."

"Illegal immigrants?"

"Mexicans, Evan. Ever hear of them? We'll be even more up to our asses in Mexicans."

"Okay, I got it," I say. "Relax, Mark. Breathe." There is a brief pause as Mark, who's visibly pissed, tries to calm down. I glance at my headphones.

"Why can't they just stay in their own country?" Mark whines. Whines. I almost laugh out loud.

"Good, Mark. What about, um, some compassion, some human kindness?"

"Yeah right, Evan. Don't you dare pretend to care about those worthless bastards." I almost respond with "No hablo ingles," but decide against it.

"Well, whatever you do, Mark," I say, pausing for a few seconds to give off the feeling I care about what I'm saying. "Don't write that into a speech." There is a shift in Mark's body, and I'm surprised to see his face lighten.

"Hey, listen, Evan. I'm human. I'm just like everybody else, okay? I'm only upset because of the crime they bring into this already wounded state. And please also bear in mind the drain they cause to our social welfare system. That's all I'm saying. Besides, everybody knows that second-generation Mexicans are all gang members...that equals more crime."

"Crime?" I ask, trying not to listen anymore ...because I simply don't care.

"Yeah, Evan. Car theft. Murder. Rape. Also bear in mind, most of them don't have car insurance, so guess who pays when they crash into my car—guess who, Evan?"

"Where's Robert?" I ask, without mentioning that young white males commit most rapes.

"Sacramento—oh shit, that reminds me. We're all having dinner at my house this week. Don't forget, very crucial. We get to listen to Robert's wife tell us all about the symbolism behind the latest quilt she's been working on. What joy. I can't wait."

"Is it raining outside?" I ask, sincerely worried. Mark shakes his head in disgust and stands up.

"Really, Evan—try to push through, okay? Get on board with reality...what does it matter if it's raining or not?" Mark leaves. I call Brooke's house and leave a message informing her that we're not going to the dinner party at Mark's house, that, "I don't think I can...deal with it."

I put my headphones back on and turn the volume up.

24

It stopped raining a couple hours ago, and I'm slightly depressed about this as I speed north on Junipero Serra Freeway at one thirty in the morning. The sky is filled with massive black clouds. My window is rolled down, the night air blitzing over me. I have the heater turned up high.

"What is the truth?" the DJ asks a female caller named Amy.

"There is no absolute truth...it's about surrealism, nihilism...I'm a priestess, don't you get that? I'm a priestess. I practice spiritual warfare," the woman explains.

"I see. How do you do that?"

"We learn to use a lot of guerrilla tactics."

"And where do you learn these tactics?"

"Our high priest teaches us, teaches us spells. He teaches us good things."

"Good things? Like what?"

"Like empathy...numerology. We trade spells."

"I'm curious, Amy. Isn't empathy in direct conflict with nihilism?"

There's a brief pause.

"Don't be so uptight," Amy says as I exit Farm Hill Boulevard and drive into the hills.

"Can you tell me more about your—what did you call it—'clan'?"

"I shouldn't…only true witches can know exactly what we do."

"Well, who can become a witch?"

I pull into Cañada College.

"Only the right people can become witches."

"Who are the *right* people?"

"You kind of have to be born a witch…no one can make you one."

"How do you know if you've been born a witch?"

I park my car in the back of the school. The campus is high in the hills and overlooks the entire valley, from parts of San Francisco all the way south toward the Santa Cruz Mountains. I turn my headlights off and stare at countless orange and white lights below. Somewhere in the vastness is a faint siren. I look for emergency lights, but can't locate any. And even though I don't want to, I think about what might have happened, where the sirens are going.

"Well, when I was young, I used to dream about flying lions and wolves. I also collected dragons and stones. I still have a lot of them. I also have a tattoo of a wolf because I love wolves. I feel a deep connection with them. It's just natural; you see…it just happens naturally. I'm going to write a book about it."

"A book?"

"Yes—about my experiences as a female witch raising children in a consumer-driven nation."

"Now let me ask you, Amy. Do you take any drugs?"

"No. I'm very healthy. I exercise a lot. I cycle every weekend on Foothill Expressway. I don't smoke or anything. I'm a clean person."

"I see. And how old are you, Amy?"

"Thirty-two."

"What do you do for a living? How do you earn money for your kids? You have children; didn't you say that earlier?"

"Yes, I have two boys—eight and ten. I'm a kindergarten teacher."

While staring at the valley, I think about highly educated men and women. I think about smog. Homeless people. Bouncers. Cries at night in the alleys and among abandoned industrial buildings. I perceive violent divorces and fury on the 280 and 101.

25

"Anxiety? What does that mean, Evan?"

"I just can't…"

"I'm supposed to tell Robert you're not coming to dinner because you're suffering from anxiety? No. Unacceptable."

"Listen to me, I'm having…difficulty feeling well."

"Feeling well? Let me tell you something. Just focus on this, okay? I have to listen to Robert's bitch-of-a-wife discuss book drives, library fundraisers, and the need for more aggressive women's rallies. So don't tell me about anxiety—"

"Try to understand…I'm…"

"You're what, Evan? What's the malfunction?"

"I'm being watched."

Silence.

"Watched? Why are you whispering?"

Silence.

"By who, Evan? Who's watching you?"

"I can't…"

"Who's watching you, Evan?"

Silence.

"I…"

"Spit it out, Evan. Who is watching you?"

"Demons. Demons are watching me."

Silence.

"Cute. You're really...a flake, Evan."

26

I'll sometimes wake up lying in my piss. I'll wake up in the night, panicked, drenched in sweat. I'll wake up to find myself screaming. Then I'll recognize certain items in the room like my bed, the clock, or a chair in the corner, and I'll begin to calm down. I'll take a Nembutal or diazepam and stand in a hot shower waiting for the sedative to hit. Afterward I'll sit in bed and look at an old photograph that my father took when I was four or five. I'll concentrate on certain aspects in the picture—attempt to relive each step of that afternoon: a flower. A road. A fracture. Guardrails. Transformers. Blue sky. Clouds. Faded yellow stripe. Trees. We were walking on an old back road in Gilroy, and he was holding my hand. He took a picture of a deer and one of me examining some small fact on the ground—some insignificant particle—a rock or maybe just an ant or insect, or maybe nothing at all.

I ran into the middle of the road and knelt down. I called out to him. I pointed to a white flower growing in the small fracture in the center of the road's faded yellow stripe. I stood up and looked around. But where were the other flowers? Did they leave it behind? What happens if we pull it out and take it to the other flowers? Death.

But if it stays here won't a car run over it? Maybe. What should we do? Tonight we can pray for it, and maybe God will take care of it. I searched along the guardrails on the side of the road. I searched for other flowers. I searched for its friends, for its parents, for anybody. In the distance large transformers hummed softly. He took a picture of the flower, and we finally walked on.

27

It's early in the evening. Mark, Robert, a few other key people, and I have been arguing about the Democratic "victories" among certain San Francisco groups for most of the day. Somehow I feel dirty. Infected. And even though I have plenty of food at the house, I end up at a store in Los Altos buying products I won't eat, merchandise I won't use—just to feel a connection to people—to feel normal.

I'm standing in the bread aisle, holding a basket in one hand and a loaf of multigrain bread in the other. A little way down from me are a woman and a young boy. I pretend to read the label on the loaf of bread while watching them out of the corner of my eye. I watch them decide on one kind of bread then walk off. They disappear around the corner. I go over to the breads they were looking at and pick up a loaf—sliced sourdough. I pick up some grape juice, which I don't drink, and in the medicine aisle I select vitamin C drops. I end up buying a box of milk bones and various canned dog foods, yogurt, frozen lasagna, iced tea, men's and women's deodorant, and soymilk. At the checkout counter, I joke with a young but decent-looking male cashier. I comment on the weather. I look straight into the young man's eyes when he hands me the receipt, but there's nothing. No connection. No feeling of bonding. And this disappoints me so deeply that I almost start crying.

28

Rain is drizzling in from the southwest, from over the Santa Cruz Mountains. The valley seems saturated. The wooden buildings in the old shopping center—where I'm having lunch with Brooke and her friend Hannah—feel drenched. Even the sidewalks and cement roads look swollen with water, ready to float away.

I watch from the bar and grill as a dog scampers across Foothill Expressway, its head low to the ground. It stops and looks back at the expressway before vanishing into thick bushes behind a large church.

I'm pretty sure I met Hannah once before, last year during a party, but I can't be sure, and it seems like too much of an effort to ask. Hannah is registered with the Green Party. Hannah doesn't eat meat. Hannah likes to talk about "saving those poor animals" and "the positive karma of vegetarianism." Hannah is mildly attractive.

"It really, I don't know, I guess—disappoints me—that so many Americans are so eager to establish so-called peace by attacking other nations. You know what I mean? There is so much, I don't know, imbalance in the world that any little thing could set it off. We could end up in world war three and end up destroying the entire human race.

For what? Cheaper oil? I just don't get it," she says in a controlled manner, then sips her tea. She smiles at Brooke.

"Really, Hannah…I think you're being a little dramatic," Brooke says. "I think we need real Christian men and women praying for our government—to help them with their tough decisions—"

"No, I really don't think so, Brooke. I mean, religion has its purposes, but there should be a clear separation—"

"I know, I know—that's not what I'm saying, Hannah," Brooke says. She looks down at her half-eaten salad, then at her water, and finally back at Hannah.

"I'm only saying that humanity can't…save itself."

I'm inwardly counting down from thirty. I'm counting the number of ice cubes in Brooke's glass of water. I'm trying to remember the number of earthquakes that strike California annually. I'm thinking about the data. The figures. The reports. Five more dead in another suicide bombing. A 4.7 on the Richter scale somewhere in Oregon followed by a 3.9 aftershock. A body found in a mall bathroom. A high school girl raped in a car on the side of the highway as hundreds of cars passed by. Three children and one adult burned to death in an apartment complex. Fifteen dead cats found in a ditch—their intestines ripped out. Ripped out. I'm trying to understand why an extraterrestrial never landed in Arizona as Colleen promised.

"You're not talking much, honey," Brooke says and touches the top of my hand. I manage to not pull away. I'm looking down at my hamburger that I ordered rare with the hope of sickening Hannah. Cooked blood and juice are draining out of the brown and pink hamburger meat, and I momentarily see myself devouring the meat greedily, lapping up the juices.

"I'm just a little tired," I say. Brooke smiles and pats my hand. Hannah sips her tea and looks out the window. I try to remember all the emergency supplies in my car: battery-powered flashlight and lantern, extra change of clothes, extra tennis shoes and boots, rain gear, fresh drinking water, AM/FM radio, spare batteries, waterproof matches, first-aid kit, toilet paper, cash, sleeping bag.

"Are you coming to *The Rocky Horror Picture Show* tonight?" Brooke asks me. I look out the window and watch the rain.

"No. I'm think I'm going to get to bed early tonight," I say after a moment.

29

That night, I wake up to strong winds rocking the house— the ceiling and walls creaking from the pressure. The room is dark and cold, and the blinds are open. I stare at the tree in the backyard. Bending. Shaking violently. I was dreaming about Brooke.

She was crying.

I don't know why.

30

Brooke is picking at her salad and saying very little. I'm drinking vodka and orange juice and trying to ignore her mood.

"How was the picture show?" I ask, pretending to be interested. Brooke looks at me, shrugs.

"It was okay, I guess. Not what I was expecting...not my crowd," she says.

After dinner, in Brooke's bedroom, I'm touching her, undressing her. She's tired and obviously not into it. She's dry when I try to enter her. She breathes in sharply, and I push harder to force myself all the way in. I'm unable to orgasm.

Later, in bed, Brooke is lying on her side. She's facing away from me, and I can tell by her breathing that she's not asleep.

"What's wrong?" I asked, bored.

"Nothing," she says, her voice withdrawn.

"I'm really not in the mood, *Brooke*. So just say it and then we can all fall asleep." There is a brief silence. I sigh loudly.

"I wish," Brooke starts, her voice breaks. "I wish you wouldn't...swear at me...during sex." I think about this for a moment. I close my eyes.

"Whatever, Brooke...are you starting your period or something?"

I tell myself I love Brooke. I tell myself I would marry her if things weren't so...confused.

It's almost ten o'clock and Brooke's asleep. My mind is heavy. Random thoughts of violence are tearing at me—snatching away the possibility of sleep. I'm annoyed I couldn't orgasm earlier. I get dressed quietly and leave without waking Brooke up to say "Good-bye."

"I can't calm these needs," a man on the radio sings as I speed south on the 280 toward San Jose, toward a destination I've been to before.

The parking lot behind the adult store is empty except for a large dumpster in the corner. I walk through the back door, the familiar smell of disinfectants and stale air impacts me. I walk down the poorly lit hallway, which opens up into a small room that has three private booths against two of the walls. Near one of the booths is an industrial mop and bucket. I glance through another door that leads to the main room where videos, sex toys, magazines and DVDs are sold. Moans pour out from the booths, and I catch the eyes of a man leaning against one of the booth doors. His eyes are bloodshot, dilated. His clothes are splattered with dirt and paint. He looks drunk, high, or both.

"Please, please," a woman's voice begs from one of the booths. The man opens his mouth slightly. Heat rushes from my stomach to my head. I stand waiting.

Anticipation. But he doesn't say anything, and I hurry into an open booth and lock the door behind me, slightly embarrassed.

The booth is small and dark. There's a small television built into the wall, protected by thick plastic. I pull a dollar from my pocket and feed it to the machine: the image of a young girl on her knees, giving a guy a blowjob in some kind of warehouse, fills the screen. The guy is holding her head, thrusting himself deeply into her mouth. She gags a little as he fills her mouth. I press a button next to the TV and a different porn scene comes on. Another man, who looks about forty, is standing in a bedroom. He's watching a woman who is lying on a small bed. She's probably in her midtwenties, but someone has put her hair in pigtails and dressed her in pink panties and a tight, pale-blue T-shirt with a sparkling unicorn across the chest. She's holding a teddy bear. The man smiles at her. The smile looks cruel, and this excites me in a sorrowful way. He walks over to her, and she looks up at him. She tries to smile seductively, but the effect is lost in too much red blush and freckles that are painted on her face to make her look young. She looks like an idiot.

"Are you ready for your birthday?" the man asks her, taking her teddy bear away.

"Are we really going on the roller coasters tomorrow, Daddy?" she asks.

The man smiles. "Yes," he says. The camera lingers on her face for too long—for a split second her eyes search the camera, and I get the impression she's somewhere else.

"Do the rides last long, Daddy?" she asks, looking at the man. But he suddenly slaps her across the face. A feeling of envy engulfs me. She doesn't scream, and this turns me on because it's an indication of how far she's come, how used to the game she is. The man turns her over and pulls her panties down to her ankles. He then puts himself inside her.

"The rides never end," he whispers in between thrusts. She closes her eyes and lets her head drop to the rainbow-covered sheets. I start to masturbate and orgasm immediately.

At my house in Los Altos, I take a long shower and some sleeping pills. I fall asleep two hours later.

31

I'm standing in the hallway of our old house in Gilroy. The sounds of a man's voice and a woman's moaning are coming from my father's room at the end of the hallway. I begin walking toward the door. As I get closer, I hear the man talking. It's my father's voice. I don't want to open the door, but the sounds from the woman are getting louder. I see my hand reach out and take hold of the doorknob. My father is saying something and repeating it, but the door is muffling the words. I turn the knob and slowly open the door. His voice becomes more and more clear. He's crying. Between sobs I can hear him whispering, "Are you immune, are you immune?" I push the door open all the way. He's sitting on the end of the bed, naked, staring at a porno movie. He's still crying and trying to get himself aroused with one hand. In his other hand is a champagne flute.

"Are you immune?" he asks me suddenly. I stare at him without answering. His face is wet, and he won't stop crying. He raises the glass up to me. I don't want to take it, but then I realize I'm holding it. I begin drinking. The woman in the porno is laughing, "Are you immune? Drink the 'maddening wine of my adulteries,'" she says. I wake up sweating. An urge to cry collides into me. I search for some sort of certainty—a feeling or idea that everything is fine. But nothing comes to me, and I feel like I'm going to scream.

32

When we first started dating, Brooke and I would sit on her dorm-room floor and look through travel magazines together. We talked about the different places we would go. We talked about the foods we would eat and the rooms we would sleep in. She showed me a picture of a beach with lots of sand and bright blue seawater. We made up an entire story about where the beach was, and how we got there, and how nobody was ever around, except maybe at night. She told me that we were lying on the beach for hours and hours listening to the ocean. She told me we sometimes kissed, but that mostly we just held hands. She cut the picture out of the magazine and framed it, then hung it up on her bedroom wall.

"To remind us to get there someday," she said.

33

"Kim from Chicago, thanks for calling the Christian Forum. What do you think about this issue?"

"Well, I agree with your last caller. I think they're all a bunch of sick perverts. I think they should be neutered and cast away."

"Well, they certainly have *something* coming. Don't they?" the male DJ says.

"These sexual predators are nothing short of animals—no feelings, no thoughts of love or mercy or even kindness. They should be locked up. We need to end the sexual perversion in America," Kim says, almost crying, "I've lived through this twice. My uncle molested me when I was seven years old. And after sixteen years of marriage, my husband left me for another woman. A younger woman."

"I'm so sorry," the DJ says quietly. "Let me ask you, Kim. Where do you think these people come from? I mean, where do you think they learn this kind of behavior?"

"I don't know. I believe some of them were victims of molestation or abuse. But I think they're a disgrace to God. They should be thrown away. God will deal with them like he dealt with Sodom and Gomorrah."

"What do you think about the pornography problem in America today?"

"Oh, it's just tragic. These men, these men who look at that trash should be ashamed of themselves. They should hang their heads in shame. Women are not objects."

"Thanks for calling in, Kim."

"You're welcome, and God bless you for the wonderful job you're doing."

"God bless you as well."

34

The sky is gray. Overcast. There is a tired breeze from the north. Brooke has not called me in almost two days.

I go into work. Mark and Robert are both there, and I don't feel like seeing or talking to either of them. I lock my office door, close the window blinds. I end up returning phone calls most of the day. During lunch, I stare at the maps on my wall—debating whether or not to call Brooke. But I decide I don't want to deal with that kind of emotion. Instead, I take an Advil and a Nembutal and masturbate in the men's room. Just before I orgasm, I think about the hippie girl who gave me the mango. I wonder if she would drive to the desert with me. I wonder if she swallows.

35

Later that night, I'm sitting on my bed in the dark, getting drunk. The alcohol is spreading through my brain, sedating me—slowly abolishing dread and guilt. Brooke has still not called or left any messages, and I'm trying not to be alarmed by this, trying not to think the worst. I push negative thoughts out of my head, but anger immediately replaces the fear. I pick up my cell phone and dial her number. I hang up before it connects. "Unacceptable, she needs to call first," I tell myself. But then guilt floods in, temporarily washing away the anger, and I dial her number again. The phone rings a few times. I picture her looking at my number on her cell phone, wondering if she should answer. I'm just about to hang up when she answers the phone.

"Hello?" Brooke asks, pretending—I'm sure of this—to not know who it is.

"Hey," I manage to say without sounding too annoyed.

"Hi." Her voice is cautious. There's a brief silence.

"What are you doing?" I ask, unable to think of anything else to say, already beginning to regret calling her.

"Just reading."

More silence. I sip the drink I'm holding. "Reading what?"

"A magazine."

Silence.

"Why haven't you called?" I ask, suddenly angry again.

"Are you drunk, Evan?"

"What are you talking about, Brooke? Why haven't you called me?" An image of her on her knees giving blowjobs to a group of men flashes across my mind. "I can't talk to you," I say.

"Evan," she says, her voice giving a little.

"No. You're not worth the effort."

"But you...called me," she says, and I think she's going to cry. "What's happening to you? You're not the same."

Silence.

"Evan? Are you listening to me?"

Silence.

"Evan?"

"What?"

"Why won't you tell me what's wrong?"

I'm looking into my drink. I tell myself it's a doorway. The drink is a doorway into oblivion, and all I need to do is walk through it.

"Evan?"

"Oh Jesus, nothing's wrong, *Brooke*."

"Evan?"

"I have to go."

"Why?" Brooke says crying. I'm briefly tempted to tell her to stop crying. I think about the girl with the great ass I saw in Victoria's Secret—a rush of pleasure shoots through me.

"Because, I just have to."

"No you don't, just talk to me—"

"You don't understand, Brooke. You don't get it, okay."

"What don't I get?" she says, choking a little. "I don't understand. Tell me, what don't I get?"

"You're really…sad, Brooke."

36

I was seventeen and it was there, at the aquarium, that he wanted to tell me about it. On the drive over, he rolled down the window and let the hot California air whip over us. We listened to the radio. I watched the horizon pass by.

I remember how easy it was to disappear there—to become hypnotized by the sea life drifting along on a manmade current. We were standing in front of the thick glass and watching the polar bears dive into the blue water, propelling themselves with their massive white paws.

"I have cancer, Evan," he said. I watched as a polar bear swam up to the surface for air. I didn't say anything because I didn't know what to say.

"What are you thinking about?" he asked me after a while. I just shrugged. I didn't really want to say. I didn't want to make him worried. I didn't want to make it worse. I didn't want him to know that I wished the thick glass would shatter—explode over us, killing us instantly—that I wanted to see tons of seawater flood the underwater observatory. I never told him this, and I guess it didn't really matter in the end anyway.

37

I look for signs of reason and clarity in my life. I search for arrangements in the motions of daily living. I listen for regularity, a pulse, but I seem unable to find any. I see my existence in glimpses—in a chain of snapshots.

I'm frightened by the odds of experiencing another bad day. I try to gain understanding—knowledge to hold onto. I sometimes pray, but the lines are increasingly blurry. I have a difficult time distinguishing between nightmare and reality. I seem unable to control my thoughts and my emotions. I'm always angry or afraid.

And as I sit at a stoplight on El Camino, I'm exhausted by the effort of trying to believe that the road is not about to liquefy and swallow my car whole.

38

Brooke has not called me in a few days, and I'm sure she's angry at me. I have to get mildly drunk before I can call her to apologize. I tell her this over the phone. There is a brief pause.

"It's okay," she says quietly. She tells me about work and as she talks, I try to picture her in my mind: dark brown hair, olive skin, and hazel eyes. I try to remember any emotional or spiritual link I may have felt with her, and I'm momentarily overwhelmed by a need to recall us at happier times.

"Were we ever...satisfied?" I ask suddenly.

Silence.

"Evan, what's happening to you?" she asks. And I think I'm going to cry, but there are no tears. I sigh.

"I don't know."

39

"Get energized."

"Hear! Hear!" The DJ says, laughing. "I'm eager!"

"Excellent—the millennials are here and so ready to live, live, live, but I want to encourage them to wait, slow down for a moment. You need to start thinking about retirement immediately, while you're still young!"

"Do you *truthfully* think young people should think about retirement while they are young?"

"Totally. Because of advancements in medicine and medical technology, people are living a lot longer. The question is do you want to work when you're sixty, or do you want to experience your dreams?"

"Yeah, good point. So what do you recommend?"

"Well, first off, I want to encourage listeners to subscribe to my podcast on how to really enjoy their retirement years. I'm going to talk a little bit now about price increases, unforeseen medical costs and, of course, bartending lessons."

Laughter.

I start to worry about my 401k and the stock market. Medicare. I'm sure it's only a matter of time before Social Security is dissolved, before healthcare goes underground and millions of people search the black market for their medications, before new policies are issued, promising everything and delivering nothing.

40

Stephanie is standing on the top of an embankment high above me. She's wearing a white tube top and pink shorts. I wave to her. She smiles and waves back. She motions for me to come up to her.

I start to climb up, but the embankment is made of dirt and it's difficult. I actually begin sweating from the exertion and have to stop to take a break after a few minutes.

"It's hard to climb," I yell up to her. She glances around, then smiles teasingly and flashes me. Her breasts are small, underdeveloped, but perky. I smile and start crawling again, but it suddenly starts to rain. The rain gets heavier, and the dirt turns to mud. I look up at Stephanie. I'm slipping. Panic.

"I'm falling," I yell up to her. She takes her tube top off, then her pink shorts, and finally her panties. She stands there, completely naked in the rain, and motions for me to keep trying. Her body is young and firm. I crawl against the current of mud. My hands are covered and the mud has splattered my clothes, but I don't care because I'm starting to get a little closer to her. The rain has turned the mud into watery slime, and I begin sliding back down the embankment again. I look up at Stephanie. "I can't reach you," I scream. She's still smiling and begins to laugh.

"I can't reach you," I scream again. She points at me, her mouth open wide in laughter. I'm sliding down faster, picking up speed. I clutch the mud, squeeze it—scrape at it with my fingers, but it seems to dissolve in my hands and I'm sliding faster and faster, and I can't figure out why I haven't reached the bottom yet.

I wake up. I'm hard. Disappointed. Angry. I go into the bathroom and look at myself in the mirror. I masturbate to the mental image of Stephanie's naked body. Afterward I fall asleep on the couch.

41

The next night, I'm driving through the Los Gatos Hills. I'm relaxed from a combination of Quaaludes and vodka. A thick fog has drifted in from over the Santa Cruz Mountains and covered the roads. I like the feeling of the fog—its thickness and its ability to utterly devour me. Make me evaporate. I turn the radio up and tell myself I could escape through the fog, through the redwood trees, along the Santa Cruz Mountains.

I call Brooke later that night. Drunk. Worried.

"I don't feel...concealed," I tell her, on the verge of tears.

"Concealed? What does that mean, Evan?" There is a pause while I think of the right words. "I'm not sure...I think there are individuals who want to...harm me?" I say, but it comes out as a question and the need to cry leaves. Brooke sighs.

"I don't know what to say, Evan." Silence. "Maybe you should start going to a counselor."

The next day, sitting at my desk, Mark calls me from his cell phone.

"Where are you?" I ask, not really caring.

"Sacramento. Never mind that—have you heard the Democrats' latest radio ad yet?"

"No."

"They're trying to make another splash. Robert wants me to write some radio ads, counterattack. What do you think, where should I hit them?" There is a long pause during which I almost hang up.

"Hello? Evan, can you hear me?"

"Yes, I can hear you."

"Well? What should I say?"

"Mark, do you ever wonder where this is all leading?"

"Where this is all leading? Evan, don't be…enigmatic. I'm trying to win us the Governor's Office."

I think about Stephanie. I think about a possible alien invasion. "It's leading nowhere," I almost say.

42

I'm leaning against the back wall of the auditorium, trying to get into the music the worship band is playing. I'm sober. I don't know why. The auditorium is large and packed with mostly college-age people. The lights are dimmed; this relieves me a little. I feel relatively safe with my back against the wall in the dark. I feel invisible. Overlooked.

Tables and chairs are set up throughout the auditorium. Standing around one of the tables in front of me is a group of four girls and two guys. I briefly think about the possibilities of a gangbang. I look at the girls, attempting to gauge how good looking they are or if they have good bodies. Their hands are raised in the air, and they are singing.

The song ends, and the lights are turned up a little. This disappoints me. A man walks onto the small stage.

"Wasn't that an awesome song? I love that one—it's one of my favorites," he says. Everybody claps. A few even cheer. The worship band leaves the stage, and the man— I think the assistant pastor—leads everyone in prayer. As people bow their heads and close their eyes to pray, I study the ass of a slightly overweight girl standing alone. She's wearing a dark colored dress that fits snuggly against her body. Her hair is long and red. Unusual. Exotic. I feel myself getting excited.

"As most of you know, Mike is out of town right now. He asked me to talk tonight. He'll be back next weekend though, and will continue with his encouraging three-part series on being single in today's world. I'm going to read out of Genesis…Genesis 3:19," he says, opening his Bible. I stay standing against the back wall. I fight the impulse to leave; I'm not sure why I should stay. I look around at the people and I feel…phony. Fake.

"In Genesis, we find God telling Adam what curses will be brought against not only the Earth but also mankind for his rebellion. Follow along if you have a Bible with you, 'By the sweat of your brow you will eat your food until you return to the ground, since from it you were taken; for dust you are and to dust you will return.' Now, as everybody knows, sin and death were introduced because of the choices Adam and Eve made…"

I leave. Not because I already know what he's talking about or because I'm indifferent, but because I feel like I'm just pretending. Just going through the motions, hoping something will rub off—hoping something will click and I'll be happy.

Later, in my bedroom, I search the Internet for porn. I download video clips of gangbangs, suck-a-thons, blackmail porn. Hours pass by. I drink vodka and masturbate half a dozen times. I think about the overweight girl from church. I use her in my mind.

43

"Do you want to grab a sandwich or something?" I ask Brooke over the phone.

"I can't. I can't leave work right now."

"What about dinner?"

"That sounds good." Silence. "I bought you something this weekend," she says. More silence. "I mean, it's nothing big, but I think you'll like it."

Brooke comes over around six. She's wearing jeans and a pink long-sleeve shirt. She hands me a wind chime.

"It's what I bought you," she says. I hold the wind chime up and look at it. "Do you like it?"

I nod.

"I'll hang it up on the tree in the backyard."

We make it through dinner without arguing. And later, lying in bed together, she rests her head on my stomach.

"I'm worried about you," she whispers.

"Don't," I say. "Don't ruin the night now."

44

I'm crawling on my hands and knees through the dark hallway of the porn shop. I crawl toward an open booth. Inside on the screen people are having sex. The floor is sticky from the orgasms of men masturbating. I begin licking the glossy fluid off the floor. I try to stop, but I can't. I keep licking and swallowing and I want to stop, but I can't walk away. I have no strength. I wake up. I'm in my bedroom. Brooke is asleep. It's three in the morning. I look at porn on the Internet for almost two hours before I'm able to fall asleep again.

45

Ten more people were killed when a man blew himself up on a crowded bus in Iraq. Two children, a boy and a girl, were among the dead. I wonder if they were related, but the article didn't say. The boy's body was torn in half.

I'm almost out of codeine.

46

The Sonoran Desert makes up 120,000 square miles that range from southeastern California through southwestern Arizona. There is a shrub that grows there called the crucifixion thorn. I feel if I could get to the desert, touch the thorn, then…things would be different for me.

In bed Brooke asks me what I'm thinking about. I tell her about the Arizona desert, about the crucifixion thorn. She tells me her friend, April, is going on a mission trip to India to help children.

"Isn't that great? I wish I could help people like that," she says.

"That's really great, Brooke." I say, but it comes out wrong. Brooke stiffens.

"Why do you do that?"

"Do what?"

"Always act like everything's beneath you…do you think you're above it, Evan?" There's a long silence.

And I'm unable to articulate to her that I'm sinking in "it" choking on "it," begging Jesus to vanish me so I don't have to deal with "it" anymore. But I seem incapable of sharing the fact that there are no obvious mountains to overcome in my life. No great hurdles to jump—that it's a matter of unconsciousness. Disbelief. Spiritual nausea. That I feel like I'm sleeping and can't wake up. I want to tell her, but don't. Because I'm not so sure I want it to stop anymore. I don't really see the point in being awake.

"You're not the only one on this planet, Evan. Everybody has problems."

47

"I can only take two quick calls, and then I must go to a commercial break. Mark, twenty-two, you're on the air. Tell us what you think about today's generation compared to past generations."

"Hi, yes. First I'd like to say I completely disagree with the last caller—today's generation might be more technologically advanced, but that doesn't mean it's better than past generations. I think today's young people are self-centered and entitled. They claim they're not, but they don't focus on important issues like creating jobs and stabilizing our economy, doing our part to end global corruption, reducing the national deficit, backing our military, solving the fossil fuel crisis, increasing voter participation among young people, things like that."

"So, you think past generations cared more about other people?"

"Yes, exactly. They were more concerned about creating a better world than about making life easier for themselves."

"Okay, thanks for calling in."

"Thank you."

"Joy, nineteen, you're on the air. What do you think?"

"Hi. I just want to say I listen to your show at work almost every day. Um, I think people shouldn't judge today's generation, calling it worse than past generations. I mean, where would we be without doctors or modern emergency equipment? Today's world has finally broken free from simple ideology and religious fanaticism. Science and education will bring true peace to this world."

"Joy, I hate to cut you off but we have to break for a commercial. Thanks for calling in."

"Okay, bye."

48

I'm lying on my bed fully dressed. My eyes are closed, and I'm trying to feel vibrations in the earth. Tremors. I try to sense the rolling waves of the Earth's surface speeding toward my house, my bedroom. I hold still and wait for the inevitable: walls imploding, two-by-fours puncturing the ceiling's skin and impaling me with sharp, broken ends. I wait for what feels like a long time, but nothing happens. I drift off to sleep.

49

Lately I've been getting drunk and searching creeks for evidence of crime. I'll look for obvious indications: torn clothing, rope, duct tape, rubber gloves, bloody clothes. Sometimes I'll find an old shoe or a child's toy, and images of violent acts will flash into my mind. Other times I'll find nothing and be extremely disappointed. Sometimes I'll just throw up half-digested vodka or simply pass out.

Mark will call my cell phone asking me where I am and say that "I'm missing too many 'coordination briefings.'" I'll walk along train tracks searching homeless camps. I'll tell him that I'm "driving to a very important meeting," I'm "in negotiations," or I'm "stuck in traffic." I examine homeless camps for used porn—with pages that stick together and reek of piss—where the chance of disease is high. Because there's something about buying a new porno magazine that's too clean…too sterilized…too packaged—a misrepresentation of its true nature.

50

He wanted to talk about the cancer—to explain why things were the way they were. He wanted to talk about the time he had left, about what I would do "after." But for the first two days on the cruise ship, we just laid out on padded lounge chairs and said almost nothing.

Later, we sat across from each other in the dining room and drank wine. I ate very little.

"Have you talked with your mother?" he asked me. I shook my head.

"I don't talk to her. You know that." I took small breaths, unsure of what he was going to say next.

"I'm going to write to her," he said after a while.

"Why?"

"Because...I want to apologize."

"Apologize? For what? Screw that crazy bitch."

"Evan."

"What?"

"She hasn't...had an easy life."

"I don't care," I said and finished off the rest of my wine. I left him sitting at the dinner table alone.

During the last days of the trip, he would sit in the hot tub or at the bar and grill. The hours were hot and long, and the sky was clear blue and seemed to never end. Sometimes he would sit next to me on the lounge chairs. I would pretend to be asleep. I would keep my eyes closed and listen to every sound possible: the ship gliding on the clear Caribbean waters, people leaning against the railing, laughing. The breeze. I focused on the sound of my breathing. I wanted to vanish into the noises.

"I just want you to know...I tried to do things the right way," he said one night in the cabin. "Do you believe that?"

"Yes."

"I wish I could have done a better job."

"It's okay. No sweat. Right?" It was quiet for a while.

"You should know...this world...has a way of murdering—"

"I don't want to talk about this. It's okay, really. I understand," I said.

I would watch him sitting at one of the patio tables on the sun deck, writing for hours. He seemed calm. Content.

We never really talked about the cancer or about why things were the way they were or about what I would do after.

51

"**N**ow's not a good time, man."

"Why not?"

"Because…I'm having dinner."

"So? I'll be quick."

There's a long, drawn-out sigh over the phone. "What do you want?"

"Nembutal."

"I'm out—don't have anymore."

"Seconal then."

"All I've got is Valium and about fifty Librium."

"Fine. Great. I'll take all the Librium and a hundred Valium."

I drive into the Santa Cruz Mountains, not far from the "hollow," and turn off onto a dirt road that leads up to the single-story house. I've been here twice before. The house is old and is not much more than a very large shed. I've never been inside, but I'm sure it's a shit hole.

I get out of my car. There is smoke and talking coming from behind the house. I walk around to the back. Sitting by a campfire are six people. Just outside the circle of people is an older fat man who's naked. He's actually naked. He's dancing slowly in place.

"Who are you?"

I turn around and look at a young woman wearing a sundress. She's holding a loaf of homemade bread.

"I'm...John." I pause then smile. She looks at me for a moment longer.

"Nice tie, John," she says, giggling and walks past me to the campfire. I look at my tie. Navy blue. A young man is playing a guitar, and I'm surprised by how good it sounds.

"Hey, I didn't hear you pull up," Tyler says, walking up to me and nodding.

We stare at each other for a split second. For the first time I realize he has blue eyes and is slightly taller than I am. He smiles and holds out a plastic sandwich bag. I give him cash. After swallowing two Valium, I put the plastic bag in my pocket.

"Cool?" he asks me. It's obvious he wants me to leave.

"I'm just wondering, why is that guy naked?"

Silence.

"Because he can be," he says, never taking his eyes off me. I nod and then walk away. Someone, maybe the guitar player, starts singing.

52

The next day the clouds have broken up, and the sunlight is bright. Instead of going into the office, I drive out to Half Moon Bay and watch the Pacific Ocean for a while. I watch as the sea swells up and crashes in a pleasing rhythm. Around noontime I take Highway 9 into Saratoga for a few drinks before going home to take a very long and hot shower. Afterward I swallow a couple of Valium down with vodka and orange juice.

Later when I'm in bed, Mark calls my cell phone three times in a row. On the fourth time, I answer.

"Hello?" I sigh.

"Evan. Where the hell are you?"

"I'm in a conference right now...can you call me back later?" I pause, and then say, "I'm trying to set up dinner with a possible financial contributor."

Long pause.

"Fine...I'll call back."

"Thanks."

We hang up. I turn my cell phone off and try to empty my head of any thoughts. Two-and-a-half hours later I fall asleep.

53

It's Saturday night, and I'm lying in bed listening to music on my headphones. Brooke walks out of the bathroom with a damp towel wrapped around her. She looks at me and says something. I rest the headphones around my neck.

"What?" I say.

"I said, you look tired."

I watch the steam float into the bedroom.

"I don't sleep well," I say. But we've been here before, and I don't mention the rest of the information—information like I only sleep for brief periods during the night despite sedatives and alcohol. Information like, when I do finally fall asleep, I'm involved in nightmares of extreme brutality. Cruelty.

Brooke drops the towel on the floor and gets into bed naked. She turns the lamp off. I feel her touch my arm, then inner thigh, teasingly. She pushes the covers back and moves down between my legs. She puts me into her mouth. I put my headphones back on and think about the hippie girl, what she would look like on all fours.

The next day, I park across the street from Foothill College and watch the girls walk out to the parking lot from campus. I think about the potential, how easy it would be. Abduction. Rape. Sodomy. Choking. Crying. Pleading—shut up and eat the apple.

54

The forecast calls for a storm with heavy rain. Already the wind has picked up from the northwest. I sit on the floor with my back against the bed and listen to the wind chime Brooke gave me—a lullaby quality. Seductive. I close my eyes and visualize dark clouds drifting inland from across the Pacific Ocean.

55

"What are you afraid of?" The DJ asks. There is a short hesitation.

"I'm afraid of...getting cancer," a male caller says.

"I see."

"I'm...afraid of pain. I don't want to be eaten alive... you know what I mean? From the inside out, the idea of sick cells devouring healthy ones...offends me."

Pause.

"I see. So it's not so much *death*...but more the *process* of dying that you're afraid of...is that correct?"

Silence.

"I don't know. I think I might be a hypochondriac."

Silence.

"I see."

There is something suggestive about the words "cancer" and "eaten alive" that makes me uncomfortable—a spiritual indication—an implication of what is happening to me. There are signs that I'm wasting away on a cross of piercing apprehension. I lurk in my house and lock the doors and windows. I miss days of work. I beg Jesus to anesthetize me. I masturbate until my skin is raw. I see and hear selectively. Connections in my mind are obscure:

You should know, this world, has a way of murdering. Do you think you're above it, Evan? It's leading nowhere. Evan, don't be an asshole. You must not eat fruit from the tree that is in the middle of the garden, and you must not touch it, or you will die. Want—to—get—off? Get dirt on anyone. Make her adore your every move. Fierce winds. Want to play with us? She will beg for more after she gets a piece. Blonde gets tag teamed. Join me for some fun with my cam. You will not surely die. Free pussy. Hot banged girls. Atoms liquefying. Bodies—in darkness—writhing against each other in agony. Shower cum on her face. Spiritual indications. Everything's different in the winter.

Piercing apprehension.

56

January slips into February. The days are sometimes cloudy and other times clear and warm. With the sunlight heating my body, I'll drive up the 280 and think about the desert and something like hope will momentarily wash over me. But always later, near evening, after I've pulled into the driveway in Los Altos, the feeling of hope will be gone and I'll be left wasted on the living room floor with an empty bottle of vodka lying next to me. I'll hold my breath and count to fifty and then exhale slowly, steadily. I'll cry bitterly. Screaming. I'll get an overwhelming need to hit Jesus across the face and then grasp him closely to me and beg him to heal me. I'll black out.

It's moments like these when the suggestion of jumping off the edge brings a smile to my face—an eroding alleviation of my mind.

57

I'm parked in the Alta Mesa Cemetery in Palo Alto listening to news talk radio. The sky is mostly clear, and there is a breeze. I roll down the window and watch a family visiting a grave. The man is pointing to a marker and the children, a boy and girl, are looking at the grave in silence. I think about the boy torn in half by a suicide bomber. I look at the little girl. I take in the details of her body. I wonder what she thinks about. I try to picture Brooke—Brooke as a young girl.

Mark calls my cell phone.

"You're missing the meeting with Robert and he wants numbers. Where are you?" I sigh. It's leading nowhere?

"Mark," I start, but something in me slips, and I lose the energy to finish the sentence. There is a short silence.

"Yes?" Mark says, annoyed.

"Just tell Robert...we're over half a million above our contribution requirement...and climbing rapidly." There is another silence as Mark takes this in.

"Really? That's great. Okay...I'll call later."

I drive to a liquor store in Palo Alto, and as I pull into the small shopping center I pass an older man holding a sign and asking for change from people leaving the parking lot. I park and make a mental note to search for another exit.

At home I start drinking and end up masturbating even though I don't really want to.

58

"Go get your mother…tell her lunch is ready," he said to me. It was August, and the heat was driving people over the edge—crime stats reaching "disturbing" levels.

"She's not my mother," I said indifferently. He sighed.

"Fine…tell *Kate* lunch is ready."

She was lying out by the swimming pool. I opened the sliding glass door, and the heat slammed into me, instantly draining energy out of me. I felt myself drifting over to her. Her eyes were closed, and she had on headphones. Her lips moved slowly—forming words I couldn't hear. Behind her, the palm tree branches sagged. Tired.

"Did you take your medication?" she asked him during lunch. He nodded. We picked at our food, and nobody said much. "Have you thought anymore about college, Evan?" she asked me after a while. I sipped a glass of water and made no indication that I even heard her. "I think people who don't go to college are selling themselves short," she said to nobody in particular.

59

"Do you like it?" Brooke asks me again. I nod yes and take another bite of the teriyaki chicken lettuce wraps. "It's a new recipe I found on the Internet," she says quietly.

I sip a large glass of red wine and try to think of something to say. But nothing comes to me. I sigh, and Brooke looks at me. She smiles weakly. I make an effort to smile back.

"It's supposed to reach the mideighties in the next couple of days," she offers. I don't say anything. "I think that's unusual for February," she says.

"What are you thinking about?" she asks. I shrug.

"Nothing really...there was an earthquake in some village in Ecuador three days ago." Silence. "Sixty people died...fifteen more are still missing."

Brooke looks down at her glass of wine. There is a brief silence.

"I didn't hear about that," she says finally.

"It's not...a big deal," I say and drink down the rest of the wine.

I fill my glass up almost up to the rim. Brooke watches me, but she seems to be thinking about something.

"What is it, Brooke?" I ask, even though I don't really want to know. She hesitates.

"Are...are you happy, Evan?"

Silence.

"Am I happy? What are you asking me, Brooke? Am I happy with our relationship? Is that it? Do you really want to start this?"

"I just—"

"No, Brooke. Bullshit." Silence. Brooke looks down at her teriyaki lettuce wraps. "*I just*," I start and Brooke looks up at me, "don't want to deal with this." I finish. Brooke looks down again. I sigh.

Later, Brooke is naked and lying on her stomach. Her legs are spread apart, and I'm inside her. Thrusting. But after a few minutes, I don't feel any closer to an orgasm. I tell her to get up on all fours, but this also has little effect. I close my eyes and think of the hippie girl. I think of Stephanie lying by the pool, and after another ten minutes, I'm finally able to orgasm. The orgasm is weak, and this angers me. I fall to my back, still hard. Unsatisfied. Brooke lies on her back and doesn't say anything.

In the bathroom I swallow two Librium. I stand in the shower with my eyes closed and try to visualize the pills dissolving in my stomach, powerful chemicals entering my blood stream.

Thick black smoke is drifting around me, making it difficult to breathe. Clarity happens slowly...the smoke is burning my lungs. I'm sitting on the ground surrounded by ashes. I want to stand up, but I'm tired. I can hear what sounds like crying, and I realize there's a man sitting on the ground across from me. His head is shaved, and he's wearing what looks like a robe. The robe has been torn. He's covered in sores, and he's looking at me. I think he's going to say something, but stinging pain suddenly registers in my brain, and I see that I'm also covered in sores. Open sores. I wake up and slowly realize I'm in Brooke's bedroom.

60

Three days later, I'm sitting in a diner on El Camino. Brooke has called to tell me she's going to be about "ten minutes late." I sip the drink I ordered and watch a teenage girl, maybe sixteen or seventeen, talking with an older woman. The woman says something, and the young girl smiles; she has long dark hair that's parted down the middle. From where I'm sitting, I can see her denim skirt. Her legs are slightly open, and I try to look between her legs but I'm unable to see anything. This both relieves me and disappoints me. An image of her naked and lying on her back suddenly flashes through my mind. Want—to—get—off?

Brooke is sitting across from me twenty minutes later.

"The gas prices are going to keep rising," she's saying.

I attempt to listen, but all I can think about is the young girl—not so much the girl as the *idea* of her: what she represents to me...an escape.

I hear myself tell Brooke, "Yeah, I heard the same thing."

61

I often drive through the Los Altos hills late at night. I search for meaning in the weather, in the wet pavement after it rains, in the darkness just beyond the headlights. I search the darkness for doorways—a way out. I find only empty roads. And this saddens me. I continually feed this sadness because it too has become an addiction for me. I seem unable to enjoy the subtlety of balance.

62

Two Librium and three shots of vodka are cascading through my body, tranquilizing my mind as I reach speeds over 85 mph in the fast lane of the 280. I'm meeting John Moore, a representative from Republicans for Environmental Protection, in San Francisco to have dinner and discuss "initiatives" that Robert Wallis will be in the position to "set in motion" if he is elected governor. Lyrics pour out of the radio: "If we could only find a way out." I turn the volume up and watch where the sun is drifting behind the westside hills. I tell myself that I can actually see the shadows growing darker among the redwood trees—spreading out over the land. And there is an overwhelming but temporary desire to drive into the mountains. "If we could only find a way out," the young man sings.

John is taller and younger than me. Midtwenties. He's wearing a white dress shirt, unbuttoned at the top, and slacks. No tie.

"Evan?" he says as I walk into the small Mexican restaurant near downtown.

"John?" I say back. I try to seem happy about "finally" getting to meet him. We order, and the waitress, a young black girl who's *okay*, leaves. Two minutes later she comes back with an imported beer and puts it down in front of me. John orders water.

"Let me just ask you right off, Evan. How passionate is Robert—no, not *just* Robert but the entire administration—how passionate are you guys about the environment?"

Something within me evaporates. Whole thoughts elapse, and I find myself disassociating from the world around me. I'm only slightly startled to hear myself say, "Very, John. Robert's *entire* administration is eager to create renewable energy resources that are truly 'pollution free,' which in turn would allow less reliance on fossil fuels. We also want to create lasting environmental laws that actually do something to help keep the environment uncontaminated. We believe better education on environmental issues needs to be taught as regular curriculum in schools. This in turn will help to create an environment that future families can enjoy. But more than that, we want to undo some of the damage already done to our environment. I'm talking about vast restoration."

I finish and polish off the beer. I motion the waitress for another one. John is nodding his agreement. He seems pleased. The talking continues, and the meal comes, but instead of eating, I order more drinks and listen to John lecture me about the state budget, better legislative analysis, how California views the environment, and the "consequences of weak agendas." He points out percentages and informs me about unnecessary spending losses. I'm starting to get drunk. I don't feel well. The restaurant is hot and more people have come in to eat. The noise level is high, and I'm surprised to just now notice this. I wipe sweat off my forehead. A small fly is cleaning itself on my burrito, and I focus on it as John continues to talk.

"Would you like another drink?" someone asks me. I look up. It's the waitress. "Would you like another drink?" she repeats. I look at her blankly. My hands are shaking.

"Excuse me...for a moment," I say and walk toward the bathroom without waiting for a response.

The bathroom is empty, and I lock myself in the only stall. My hands are still shaking, and I stare at them for a moment. I'm having difficulty breathing, and I think I'm going to pass out, but instead I throw up.

I wash my face and hands then take a Librium or codeine, I'm not sure which, and swallow it. I open the bathroom door and look out. The noise of the restaurant rushes in, and my heart begins to beat faster. I shut the door. I count to fifty, then open the bathroom door and walk out of the restaurant.

Outside, the night sky is clear. I turn the radio up and drive around the city until I finally start to calm down. Sometime later I end up in a club that's packed with goths. Heavy underground metal is blasting over the sound system as I pay the bartender eight dollars for a small Styrofoam cup of vodka and orange juice. Down from me are two girls dressed all in black. They look up at me occasionally and laugh. I sip my drink and try to determine if they're good looking. Their faces are painted white—dark reddish lipstick. One of the girls walks over to me, and I feel adrenaline rush from my brain into my stomach. Anticipation. Want to get off?

"Are you orporate shout?" she asks, but the music is so loud that I can't understand her.

"What?" I shout back. She leans in close. I feel myself getting hard.

"Are you a corporate sellout?" she repeats and looks at me. I stare at her. My mouth is dry. She's laughing now, and I feel myself pushing through people, running for the door.

63

I'm lying on my bedroom floor in the dark. Naked. A porno that I've already watched four times is playing soundlessly on the computer.

"'My heart is in anguish within me,'" a man on the Christian radio station is saying. I stare at the ceiling and attempt to empty my mind of anything but his voice. I close my eyes and imagine I can actually see his voice coming out of the radio—penetrating my mind. "'The terrors of death assail me. Fear and trembling have beset me; horror has overwhelmed me. I said, oh, that I had the wings of a dove, I would fly away and be at rest—I would flee far away and stay in the desert.'"

64

Later in the week, unusually warm gusts from the southwest rip through the Bay Area, reaching speeds of 35 mph and raising temperatures to the mideighties. I stand for a long time at my bedroom window and watch the tree in the backyard. Shaking violently. Wind chimes. Fear in me. Apprehension. A teenager pulled out of his car and thrown into the fast lane after a small fender bender that was, according to CHP, the result of "someone talking on a cell phone." Art Jovita, thirty-two years old, walked downtown to buy "something sweet" to celebrate the news that his wife was finally pregnant. But somewhere along the line, something went wrong, a miscalculation and he's dragged behind a SUV and then beaten to death. The take is roughly fifteen dollars. "That's all the money he had...he wanted something sweet," his wife told the police. No suspects. More money. More power. More pleasure. Weakening rushes, increase the dosage. And the tree is bending and bending and bending, and I'm sure it's going to snap. I clench my jaw and watch expectantly. The Librium in my body tries to assure me that everything's going to be okay. If we could only find a way out. But I doubt. I doubt you, God. Why have you made us? I would have been better off uncreated. Please be real, God. Please...show up.

65

Brooke is asleep in my bed. She's breathing slowly and I watch, temporarily hypnotized, as her chest slowly rises and falls. I swallow a Librium with wine and turn the volume up on my headphones. Calming electronic waves fill my mind, and I close my eyes.

I remember going to a beach in Half Moon Bay with Brooke last year. I'm able to envision, actually *feel*, the warm sun. Toward evening we watched the vast Pacific horizon slip further and further away from the sun; the apprehension in me rendered temporarily meaningless.

66

"Uh, yeah...hi...this is John. I just wanted to see if you're okay or what...you kind of left me there...I'm not sure I understand why you left the restaurant without, I don't know, without saying anything I guess. I paid for the meals...and drinks. Did you get sick or something...I'd appreciate a call back if you get the chance...okay."

There are two other voicemails from John and a number where he can be reached. I delete all the messages without writing the number down. I don't call him back. I'm just unable to face it.

67

In my mind, fantasies murmur with increasing intensity. Chemicals are released; endorphins ease the staggering pain of consciousness, of the headlines, of the grotesque nightmares. It's becoming more difficult to walk away from the fantasies. The days seem to merge—I drive for hours and hours with no destination. I wake up during the night, and Brooke will be asleep next to me, but I won't remember how she got there. And somewhere between reality and fantasy, I bought three hundred dollars' worth of painkillers from Tyler.

It's late February. The heat wave has passed and a cold front has moved in.

68

We're speeding across the sky in an airplane. The evening sky is a severe pink and purple. She pushes the throttle deeper, and I feel the plane surge forward, gaining momentum.

"Where are we going?" I ask. She reaches over and slowly caresses my hand.

"Nowhere," she says quietly. Her voice seems to resonate in my mind, my stomach. "We're going nowhere."

I rest my head against the seat and close my eyes.

"I want this...forever," I say, but the words are only in my mind. Even though my eyes are closed, I'm able to feel the plane dive. I'm able to feel the rush as we fall. And just before impact I open my eyes and look at her and I get the impression she's not a real person but the essence of my need.

I wake up in bed. Alone. I walk into the bathroom and swallow two codeine and watch myself in the mirror as I masturbate—transfixed by the slow deliberate motion of my hand sliding up and down. I imagine myself falling. Rush.

69

"**Y**ou're missing too many meetings," Mark informs me over the phone.

I don't respond. Strong winds push across the large apricot orchard where I'm parked. I turn the page of a porno magazine I took from a homeless camp three weeks ago. The pages are stiff. Brittle. And this awakens something in me.

"Hello...are we communicating with the world today, Evan?" I sigh.

"Missing too many meetings...I'm aware of this."

"I'm sick of answering to Robert for you—the combined missteps," he stops.

I study a series of pictures where a young blonde on her knees is smiling up at a guy who is emptying his orgasm all over her face.

"Are disastrous, Evan." Mark finishes.

I feel myself getting hard. I imagine the girl in the airplane. I picture her on her knees smiling up at me as I—

"Get the mismanagement...resolved. Oh yeah, Robert wants a financial update. What's the projection for February month-end?" Mark says.

I turn the page: same girl licking orgasm off her mouth. My mind feels set on fire. "We're 25 percent above the goal."

"Twenty-five percent. Good. We need to discuss potential—"

I close my eyes and think of the girl flying the plane into nothingness. I tell myself we're speeding through the sky together. To nowhere…the effect is surreal.

70

It rains sporadically during the last days of February and into early March. I spend greater amounts of time in dark porno booths, drinking from a pint of vodka, listening to my headphones—building an illusion—a fantasy world so strong that my only desire is to climb through and disappear. Forever.

And more frequently, after I've masturbated, at the instant I feel myself orgasm I will briefly be released from an overwhelming heaviness...a momentary understanding. And I will get a glimpse that this illusion isn't really about sex but about something else. Something deeper...a transcending need.

Brooke calls and leaves a message just wanting to, "Say hi...you haven't called in a while. You feel...distant, Evan."

71

I'm woken up at two in the morning from nightmares of governments collapsing, of landslides decimating entire villages, of newborn babies tortured, of fallen angels raping my body as I beg for mercy. I'm woken up by the sound of my screams.

I swallow a codeine and Librium and take a long shower. Afterward I drive along Skyline Boulevard with the radio turned up loud. During a commercial break, there's a news report and "authorities discovered the body of a young man in a university dorm room after an anonymous phone call yesterday. They believe he committed suicide. In a short letter found on his laptop, he mentions a class on naturalistic evolution and a booklet called *The Humanist Manifesto*. Although no official cause of death has been given, there is speculation of an intentional drug overdose. No statement has been given by the university."

I change the radio station, and a song I like is playing. I merge onto the 280, allowing my mind to imagine the details of the death: him confused, breathing rapidly, passing out, lungs filled with vomit.

72

The sky is a bright blue some days. I sit in the Cañada College parking lot, overlooking the vastness of the Bay Area below, and watch the white clouds drift along the horizon. I drink vodka while the full weight of a need I don't understand slowly crushes me.

73

Camera comes into focus: there is a young student holding a black cordless phone to his ear.

Professor: "What were you trying to accomplish in your paper?"

Student: "I don't really know…a sense of continuity, a sense of flow in the way things are…I guess."

Professor: "What do you mean?"

Student: "I'm not sure. I guess I was hoping to discover a sense of meaning."

Professor: "Why did you title your paper 'A Voice Calling Out'?"

Silence.

Student: "Um, I guess because I don't feel like there is anyone really there, you know, in the universe…I was hoping to discover a meaning-to-it-all value."

Professor: "Are you religious?"

Silence.

Student: "No."

Professor: "Do you realize that your title is a biblical reference?"

Student: "Yes."

Professor: "I understand your sense of uncertainty. That's just the way it is. We have come too far in our consideration of the universe…you understand…we simply can't hold onto the old belief systems. You must put your hope in technological advancement, you must accept the universe is an accident…you understand what this means?"

Silence.

Student: "Yes. It means the universe is empty."

Camera zooms in on the student, alone in a dark bedroom.

Student: "I feel lost…I don't feel like I belong anywhere."

Professor: "It's just something you are going to need to accept."

Student: "Am I really only matter…am I only chance, an accident?"

Professor: "We all are. You are not alone in this."

Camera zooms in closer on the student. He's crying quietly now. He holds the phone to his ear and walks into a bathroom. Camera follows slowly behind him. He opens a prescription bottle of pills and dumps them onto the counter. The director whispers something to the cameraman, and the cameraman nods and pans down to the pills on the counter. He swallows one pill. Then two. Then six. Then fifteen. Through the phone the professor says something to him and he answers, but his voice sounds distant and he's crying.

Student: "I feel lost...I don't feel like I belong anywhere."

Professor: "Would you feel happier believing a lie... you must accept that there is no voice calling out. There is nothing."

Camera fades away from him. Darkness slowly overtakes the room.

I wake up suddenly. I'm in bed, and the blankets are on the floor. The room is cool. Dark. The digital clock shows 1:30 a.m. It's still raining outside. I lay still and listen to the rain.

74

I open my eyes, and my father is sitting in the lounge chair next to me. He's holding an open champagne bottle on his stomach and looking out across the swimming pool. And even though he's wearing dark sunglasses, I can sense he's been crying. He drinks from the bottle, and after a while, I stand up, my shadow covering his body. I turn the volume down on my headphones.

"Happy birthday," I say, my voice surprisingly uninterested.

There is a long silence, and I fight the urge to leave. He looks up at me. I take my headphones off. He doesn't say anything and looks back at the pool, at something beyond the pool. Something I'm unable to see. All his hair is gone from the chemo. I put my headphones back on and walk away.

75

"I have no idea what that means, you know...even now... I can feel the hollowness of everything, you know? I can *feel* the hollowness of everything I see around me...I don't think there's a clear definition for us...for what a man should be."

"I see...and how long did you say you've been married, Donald?"

"Fifteen years."

"Do you have children?"

"Two boys."

"How does this...lack of *definition* affect your relationship with them?"

"I don't really know, I guess I feel...bored with them, you know? Angry."

"I see. Are they aware of this? Do they know this?"

"I don't know...maybe they can feel it...I don't care. I no longer fear exposure."

"I see. Thanks for calling in, Donald."

"Okay. Thank you. I love your program."

76

The dance club is empty and totally dark except for a single flashing light that slowly changes from red to blue to purple. I feel myself being drawn out onto the dance floor. The light is pulsating soundlessly, and I realize I'm standing in the desert. It's windy. I see what looks like someone crouching, and I move closer. It's a young woman sitting on the edge of a large cushion. She's leaning over, hugging her knees. Her long hair, partially illuminated by the light, is blowing in the wind. She's so quiet. I feel a deep need to talk to her, to touch her...to be where she is.

She's wearing a shoulder-less black dress and no shoes. "Are you real?" I ask.

She looks up at me but doesn't seem to really see me. The light is changing colors faster and her gaze is distant, her mouth slightly open. Wet. She's holding an apple, and there is a bite taken out of it. I see my hand lift the apple out of her hand and raise it to my own mouth. I bite in deeply, juice shooting into my mouth.

I'm falling through utter darkness, and I feel a gust of wind. I open my eyes, and I'm lying on the desert sand. The young girl is still sitting on the cushion. I try to stand up, but nausea overwhelms me and I begin to throw up pornographic images. I vomit up the thousands and thousands of orgasms I've spilled out in desperate attempts to reach something beyond the physical rush of pleasure.

I wake up. I stare at the ceiling. Frustration crashes through me. The knowledge, that real connection...unadulterated connection in this life, a relationship free from all deterioration, pride, fear, is...impossible.

77

"What are you thinking about?" Brooke asks me.

"Nothing," I say, without opening my eyes.

"You feel distant, Evan."

I open my eyes, my head slightly spinning from alcohol. Brooke is standing next to the bed, pulling her panties up.

"Stop saying that," I sigh.

"Stop saying what, Evan? Distant? Why don't you like to talk with me anymore?" I can hear her voice break. I close my eyes. "You're not the same," she says, crying now. "You've changed, Evan."

"Stop saying my name, Brooke. I know my name, Brooke."

"I don't understand you...are you angry at me for something? It's like you're always annoyed with me."

I sigh. Fantasies begin stirring—taking me away.

"I don't feel any emotional link with you anymore," Brooke says, sniffling. There is a long silence, and I'm driving along a road in the desert with Stephanie and—"Evan?"

"What?"

"What's wrong with you, why don't you talk to me?"

"Because." I picture Stephanie smiling at me. Encouraging me.

"Are you still attracted to me?"

"Because...I hate you," I say and open my eyes. Brooke is looking at me. Her eyes are red. She doesn't say anything. She just starts crying.

"Why do you hate me?"

I stare at her for a moment and then close my eyes.

"I don't know."

78

I'm naked. Around me, circling me, is a group of men who are also naked. They are all masturbating. One of the men behind me is whispering "Yes" over and over. I suddenly realize I'm on top of a woman, shoving forcefully into her. She's naked except for a ripped dress that's hanging from her waist. Her bra has been torn off her body, leaving dark bruises on her skin. Blood is flowing from her mouth and nose. She's whimpering. Crying. Her eyes are wide, pupils dilated. Shock. One of the men suddenly moans loudly and orgasms. I feel pleasure building up inside me, gaining power, and I begin to push into her faster, feverishly. I want to erupt deep inside her, but what seems like a long time passes and I'm unable to orgasm, and I don't understand. I stand up. Tired. Confused. Another man immediately climbs on top of her. He spits in her face. I start to leave, and one of the men stops masturbating and looks at me. He's grinning.

"It's leading nowhere," he says.

And I wake up sweating. Cold. Hard. I masturbate, and for a split second after I orgasm, things become clear for me. Messages make it through. I become aware of certain facts about myself. Correlations in my mind are made.

With every passing scene, every orgasm spilled in a dark booth, something terrible is confirmed and reconfirmed, a severe lie that I can't quite name, an ever-increasing rush of insanity. Intoxicating. I'm getting off on the unconceivable. And I'm sure it's only a matter of time before I crash.

I swallow a Librium and put on my headphones. I wait for reality to bring me back from the burning idea that freedom waits for me in suicide.

79

I'm half an hour late to a meeting with Mark and Robert—stuck in traffic on the 280. I'm on three Librium, and I am having trouble focusing on what needs to be done. The radio is a never-ending siege of commercials. I turn it off and try to clear my mind of anything negative. In the lane next to me is a van. I try not to look; attempt not to notice that it's an older van. I attempt to convince myself that the van is not filling me with fear. Uneasiness. But I can't ignore the fact that the van is sanded in some places and not in others—that what's left of the paint, a reddish color, is faded so badly that it actually looks like someone painted it with rust.

The van pulls ahead of me a little. I don't want to look at the driver. White male. Images tear into my mind: the van is not filled with dead bodies. This is only a lie. There is not a young girl chained to the floor of the van, naked, bleeding, and unconscious. I'm not getting off. I'm not savoring the details—I'm disgusted and tormented by the idea of a young girl being abducted and cruelly raped, murdered, and then casually dumped into a dumpster. My hands tighten around the steering wheel. I feel dizzy. Sick.

I can't seem to catch my breath. My cell phone rings, and I pick it up without checking who it is.

"Evan," Mark says. And I almost blurt out "wrong number" and hang up.

"Yes."

"Where are you? Robert is sitting in the conference waiting for you. *Waiting*, Evan. Unacceptable."

I begin searching for an exit.

"There are indications that I can't...ignore...indications that I'm not well," I say, surprised to hear my voice break.

"Listen, Evan, I. Don't. Care. Get here now."

"I don't think I can stay here...like this...any longer."

"Stay where? What are you talking about, Evan. Huh? What are you talking about—"

I hang up and turn the phone off as I exit the highway.

I get back on the 280 and head southbound.

80

It's the afternoon when I wake up. The hotel room is cool. I take a couple Librium and stand in the shower letting warm water run down my neck and back.

Afterward, I stare out the window. I focus on the point where the sky converges into the empty desert horizon. It's windy, and a large dust cloud forms then moves across the dirt parking lot. I think about Stephanie. I try to picture her lying by the pool. I try to see her face, her eyes. I watch the dust cloud pass the small pool at the far end of the parking lot and head out into the open desert. Near the pool is a large thermostat. It reads 83°F.

Later, sitting on a lounge chair by the pool, I listen to music on my headphones. Librium comforts my mind into a trance-like state. I close my eyes and breathe in the dusty gusts of wind. When I open my eyes later, the sun is setting and the clouds in the sky are bright pink. An older woman is sitting in the shallow end of the pool, resting her head along the pool's edge. Behind her a little boy, maybe four or five, is spinning in circles. He's wearing a T-shirt with cowboys printed all over it. I try to remember myself at that age. Another gust blasts through, rippling the blue pool water. I fight off an urge to cry…to scream.

The days melt away. I sometimes sit in the room watching porno movies on cable and drinking vodka mixed with Librium pills that I watch dissolve in the alcohol. I'll sometimes wake up in the middle of the night, still drunk, lying in my vomit. I'll take a shower. Afterward, I'll turn on the radio and listen to late-night programs and pretend I'm not really alive. I'm only a scene in a movie.

"Where are you?"

"I'm...nowhere," Stephanie says distantly.

I open my eyes to brilliant sky. Stephanie is lying on the lounge chair next to me. She's wearing a men's black button up shirt and black bikini bottom. The shirt is open, revealing part of her young breasts and stomach. She looks away from the pool and smiles at me.

I hear myself asking, "Are you real?"

"I'm nowhere," she says teasingly. I'm crying.

"What's happening to me?"

She smiles, and I want to reach out and touch her, but there is no strength in my body. I can't sit up.

"Don't you want me, Evan...don't you want to get off?" she says giggling.

"When will I be...satisfied?" I mumble. Stephanie is gone.

Thick black smoke is drifting around me, making it difficult to breathe and clarity happens slowly...the smoke is burning my lungs. I'm sitting on the ground surrounded by ashes. I want to stand up, but I'm tired. I can hear what sounds like crying, and I realize there's a man sitting on the ground across from me. His head is shaved, and he's wearing what looks like a robe and the robe has been torn. He's covered in sores, and he's looking at me. I think he's going to say something, but stinging pain suddenly registers in my brain and I see that I'm also covered in sores. Open sores. I touch one, and pleasure detonates fiercely through my mind and into my stomach. After the pleasure subsides, the sore gets more painful. I touch it again, and more pleasure shoots through me, cooling the pain. But the pleasure isn't as intense and the pain is getting worse. Soon I'm rubbing different sores, sticking my fingers into them, trying to keep the pleasure going, but the pleasure is fading, and the sores are bleeding now. I ask the man sitting next to me for help, but he's scraping at his skin with broken pottery. I want to talk to him, but I'm too tired...I can't form the words. I look down at a piece of pottery in the burning ash...I look down at the piece of pottery for a long time.

I wake up. I'm lying on the motel floor. Naked. Sweating.

81

"Time does not exist here," the words in the magazine say. Below the faded red letters is a picture of a young couple relaxing in lounge chairs. Spread out before them is a large swimming pool. The woman is looking up at a waiter. The waiter is holding two drinks. They are the only people in the picture, and I can't help but wonder where the other guests are. The man sitting next to the woman is looking away at something beyond the range of the picture's vision. I found the magazine in an abandoned trailer, thirty-seven miles south of the motel. I have been visiting the trailer periodically, drawn by some indication in the strangeness of its being there. I study the ad for a moment before looking back at my empty drink. I watch as the ice slowly melts in the bright morning sun. I look for imperfections in the ice—cracks—a lack of consistency in shape. Contradictions.

"Absolutely not," a man's voice says casually over the radio. "Let's not forget the tenacity and resourcefulness of Robert Wallis's campaign team. The sudden resignation of Evan Rand is one of any number of unexpectancies that can happen and have happened to individuals running for public office."

"Has Wallis's campaign chosen a new chief fundraiser?"

"The last I heard from Mark Schnell's assistant was that they were looking at some very promising leads. Although nothing is official, there was the mention of Alan Colwell, a graduate of Stanford—a promising up-and-comer among conservative groups."

"Do you know any more about Evan Rand's resignation?"

"Well, it certainly had nothing to do with the campaign or how it's being run. The press release issued two days ago by Wallis's PR director stated 'personal reasons.' Beyond that, I can only speculate..."

"Would you call Rand's actions 'irresponsible,' given the timing of his departure?"

"You'd have to ask him."

"What do you see down the road for Robert Wallis's political career?"

"If you're asking about any White House aspirations, I'd tell you that anything is possible."

A small pool of condensation has formed around the bottom of my glass.

82

"I feel like...a disaster...a spectacle for people to watch..."

"Why are you telling me this?"

"I need to talk with the hippie girl...the one holding the mango."

"What are you talking about, man?"

"I feel uninhibited in certain settings..."

"I don't know what you're talking about man, uncool."

"I need to talk to the hippie girl."

"You're crazy. I already told you there is no one like that, man."

"She can save me."

"No, man. You're insane."

"She gave me the mango."

"You're insane."

"Stop saying that."

"You're insane. *Insane*...don't call here anymore. I mean it."

83

Time does not exist here…the incantations of the desert. The force of thirty-mile-per-hour wind evaporates my sense of continuity, of stability. Sometime between breakfast and lying out by the pool—maybe an hour, maybe two days, maybe three weeks—I find myself standing inside the abandoned trailer again. I stare out a shattered window at a small aluminum boat, lost to the hot dust, burned, rusted, no oars, no motor, no power of movement. Debris is scattered around the boat: ripped tires, half a surfboard, canned food. Just beyond the trash is a crucifixion thorn. I stare at the tall bush: still, calm. The shadows of clouds are moving slowly over large rock faces in the distance. I briefly take in the easy movement, then look back at the inside of the trailer: old newspapers, magazines, a few pieces of clothing, and a broken walker. I move into the small room in the back. The wall paneling is gone. The room is empty except for a stained carpet, a pile of garbage in one of the corners, and an office chair with the leather and padding cut away.

I sit in the chair and wipe dust off my forehead and mouth. I pick up an old astrophysics book I discovered the last time I was here. I open the book and take out a badly decayed Polaroid. In the picture is a middle-aged man holding a baby in his arms. He's standing in a living room, not a trailer. I stare at the picture—at one time a point of reference for somebody, maybe the middle-aged man, I don't really know, but now lost...forgotten.

Driving away, I glance in the rearview mirror and watch the trailer and boat get smaller, a broken sign of purpose now abandoned, vanishing. I turn on the radio, roll down the window, and try not to look back.

Later, out by the pool, I watch a man lying in a lounge chair, holding a beer. Next to him is a portable radio—the voice of some faceless person drifts out of the small speaker, moving along the desert air.

"There are no easy answers..."

"Why did you call today's program?"

"I can't seem to accept the resignation in my mind..."

"Do you have any children?"

"It seems impossible, even to look at...I have stopped trying to take in details...the lines on the map are obscure to me...I'm just...drifting...it seems to be the only thing I can hold onto anymore...the motion of drifting, it's the only thing tangible...fixed."

"What about food, bills, retirement?"

"There must be a way out, a way through. More than escapism. Clearness. Connection. Purpose."

"How did you get to this place...this need for clearness?"

"There are no easy answers…"

"Why did you call today's show?"

"I'm looking for a certainty beyond the motion of a purposeless drifting…I need more than the coalescence of accident, of history, of thought, of intention…I need a point of reference that exceeds my need for a point of reference…something that calls me out…something that encourages me to push through the impossibility…something that calls me by a volition transcending the impossibility that the finite is all there is."

I put on my headphones and close my eyes. I think about the man holding the baby. Time does not exist here.

84

The heavy dark blue of the sky is fading into light pink and pale blue near the horizon.

"Where are you?" Brooke asks over the phone.

"The Sonoran Desert," I say, watching the sun drifting slowly closer to the edge of the horizon.

"The desert..."

"I'm staying in a motel...in the desert."

There is a brief silence.

"When are you coming back?"

Silence.

"Do you think I should come back?"

"Yes."

The sky and desert converge on a distant point, and there the sky seems colorless; a place of possibility that I am unable to reach.

85

"**K**evin from Washington, DC, you're on the air. Go ahead."

"Yeah, hi...I guess if I could ask God a question...I guess I would ask...to what end—to what end do you strive, God... the love of God; what for...where is the cross leading?"

"How old are you, Kevin?"

"Fifty-four."

"What do you think God would say?"

"I don't know...I don't really care...I must find my own happiness...I have to make my own hope...I am untouched by the effort of God...by the words of God's story...I don't accept it."

"You don't accept what?"

"I don't accept the concept of God."

I turn the radio off and stare out the window. The expanse of desert is somehow calming, reassuring. I focus on a point along the distant horizon and try to imagine Brooke, attempt to form her in my mind.

How did I get to this place...a question for you, God... where am I going...is there something more than longing...is there such a thing as touching you...the actuality of you?

I must find my own happiness…I have to make my own hope…I am untouched by the effort of God…by the words of God's story…I don't accept the concept of God—the incantations of manmade reason, dizzying ambiguity, the listless oblivion of all axioms.

Are you there, God?

Are you listening?

86

Jesus wept.

87

"**O**pen your eyes, Evan."

Silence.

"Don't you want me, Evan? Don't you want to get off?"

Silence.

"Open your eyes, Evan."

Silence.

I open my eyes. I'm standing in the aisle of an airplane. Stephanie is standing in front of me, and she is naked. She's smiling. The air is cool, and I can smell the salt air of the ocean.

"Don't you want me? Don't you want to get off?" she asks, still smiling.

"Can you help me?" I hear myself ask.

She starts giggling, and I realize that I'm not wearing any clothes, and behind me is an impossibly long line of men who are also naked. Although I can't see the door, I am able to tell that it is open and as I am pulled out into darkness, I can hear the man who was standing behind me asking, "Can you help me?" I try to look down, try to determine how high up I am. When I look back up at the plane, I can see the other men are falling after me into the night air, into emptiness.

88

It's one in the morning, and I am looking at an old photograph of Brooke that I found in my wallet. She is wearing a midnight-blue dress and smiling at the camera. I think I took the picture at someone's wedding, and I am surprised by how difficult it is to remember that day and whose wedding it was. Brooke looks happy, and I stare into her face, trying to remember her. I study her smile and her cheekbones, and her hair. I remember us going to the movies together. I remember driving up the coast and into San Francisco for dinner. I remember it being easy, being good, being clean. I remember craving her attention. And as I look into her face, I try to remember how I first started to hate her. But I am unable to recall how or why. Sorrow for her—for her person, her thoughts, her voice, her existence—wells up in my chest and surges through me.

89

Severity. Floating. Eastern winds. Pale blue. Shatterproof...I find my terror there, exacted on the horizon. An ever-present cancer that is sometimes transitory and other times undeviating. Unblinking. I will wake up at 3:00 a.m. and realize it's not a single moment in my life that terrifies me, but rather, an infinite darkness of uncompromising ideologies, doctrines... a brokenness in mankind. I will wake up at 3:00 a.m. and see fragments of this brokenness in my peripheral vision—in snapshots of the past. I will wake up at 3:00 a.m. and remember my father. The cancer killed him when I was nineteen. He was buried in Los Gatos. It was spring, and the leaves of the birch trees in front of their house in Los Gatos were young and bright green. After the funeral, I walked around the cemetery for an hour listening to music, watching the shadows of clouds driven by strong eastern winds moving slowly across the manicured cemetery lawns.

"This world has a way of murdering. What are you thinking about? Are you immune? I'm going to write her because...I want to apologize. Tonight we can pray for it, and maybe God will take care of it. I wish I could have done a better job."

I will lay on a lounge chair by the motel's swimming pool. I will watch clouds drift across the sky...pushed by eastern winds, the warm air crashing over me. I will close my eyes and listen to the wind. When I open my eyes, the sun will be setting, the sky a severe pale blue and pink. In the evening the winds blow harder, and I will look out the window. It is, in the evening, in the night, where the anchor dissolves, even the false hope of manmade reason fails, a place where I am set adrift into emptiness. In my mind an utterance slowly forms—a bewilderment grasped in the silent annihilation of all meaning. I am troubled by certain words...words like "normal," "a normal life." I am troubled by empty intellectual promises, by the peculiarities of myself. I am troubled by the grinding words that penetrate the night. I am troubled by the realization that my life is a matter of unconsciousness—an ever-deepening numbing brought on by the slow expansion of insanity. I live in a world where every effort is made to escape into illusion. I am chasing after these illusions, these hollow assurances, propelled by a reality that seems as equally insincere. It is in the night that a growing awareness calmly overtakes me—a reading between the lines in which I begin to recognize the brokenness of mankind as simultaneously subtle and brutal.

I will move along, trying to ignore the purpose of governments, prisons, hospitals, and mental institutions. I will walk among people, hear them talk, enveloped in the same atmosphere of sunlight or cloudy skies. I will sit in a restaurant and see them order a meal and a drink. Laughing. And I will have difficulty shaking the thought that, given a momentary shift in circumstance, we could be killing each other.

And there, floating on my back, I can see the expanse of mankind spill out before me—contrasting colors colliding and bleeding into each other: apathy, nihilism, hate, torment, dread...acute anxiety gushing into compassion, love, laughter, peace, and calmness. What is this place... this earth...this humanity?

The questions persist. I try to tell myself I'm shatterproof, but I still sense a longing, a need for reassurance, purpose, something to hold onto—effecting a kind of slowing down where soft colors gently lull me into a place of quiet illumination—clean oceans of blue. Warm sunlight. It is in this quiet illumination that I will remember the stories I read as a child: *Where the Wild Things Are*, *Peter Rabbit*, *Alice in Wonderland*, *Winnie the Pooh*, *The Cat in the Hat*. It is also in my childhood that the first colors of tacit danger appeared, symbolic imagines of fear—vampires, werewolves, unnamable monsters—implications of real terror, a glimpse into an underlying current that flows beneath the surface of mankind. A momentary shift in circumstance, and I perceive these vampires, werewolves, unnamable monsters—unveiled—homicides, school shootings, gang rape, assault and robbery, carjacking, aggravated burglary, drug overdose, arson, runaways, the dejected, abused, sickly, insane. I perceive a darkness in which childhood stories disintegrate. Swallowed up. I perceive the shock found in mankind...this is the place where my feet slip, where my mind staggers; I am left to waste in manmade nightmares.

I will try to remember cotton candy, sleepovers, watching Pinocchio or Mary Poppins. I will try to remember my father's beehives: the thick, deliberate honey on my tongue. Riding bikes, building forts, and exploring the creek. Thanksgiving. The glittering effect of Christmas lights. Easter...hypnotized by clean white eggshells submerged into violet, crimson, amber, emerald. Sky. I will remember California summers: lying on the edge of a pool, my hand floating in the cool water, watching the pale blue water ripple in the breeze. A momentary shift in circumstance: the ground dissolves beneath me, and I wake up at 3:00 a.m. A sense of falling...intellectual vertigo brought on by haphazard dogmas, slogans, watch words: cultural identity, fatalism, lost generation, Marxism, capitalism, acid rain—a sort of social schizophrenia where clarity becomes obscured. I wake up at 3:00 a.m. suffocated by the realization that transcending joy and the uttermost brokenness are both found in the nature of mankind. I wake up at 3:00 a.m. and comprehend frustrating answers: a subtle awareness of God's calling out, sometimes transitory and other times undeviating. Unblinking. I wake up at 3:00 a.m. and feel the need to see a place of true clarity, to realize and touch an intimacy that exceeds the human experience. But I am continually swallowed by the subtly of false appearances…a slipping down that is sedating, warm, unregistered by caution, inviting. A slipping where the stomach momentarily soars, the heart races and the need for greater rushes, for uncontained depravity, whispers and calls the mind with heavy promises of connection, of clarity, of relationships that are undisturbed by the disjointed movements of life…a promise of escaping myself.

I'm searching for a connection with God.

90

I drop a painkiller into the vodka and orange juice, and then another and another and another. I close my eyes and try to imagine the pills dissolving into the crisp, orange liquid. I sip the drink and listen to strong winds sweeping over the motel parking lot. I briefly stare out the window into the desert, into the blue sky. I imagine myself driving away. The desert highway is straight and except for the eastern winds, quiet. And as I drive toward California I think about the man in the photograph that I found in the trailer. I wonder if the trailer was his, if he lived there, in the desert. I wonder if he found what he was looking for.

91

"In other news, the body of Evan Rand was discovered two days ago in a motel in the desert. Mr. Rand was the chief fundraiser for Robert Wallis, the Republican candidate in California's gubernatorial race. Mr. Rand recently resigned from the campaign for personal reasons. Authorities are not certain but believe Mr. Rand died from a drug overdose. Authorities don't know if the overdose was accidental, but speculate..."

Epilogue

"**H**ow do you think you got to such a place...not just the nightmares and violent thoughts but all of it?"

Silence.

"The way I lived before I accepted God, or even the idea of God, was...*is*...deeply ingrained...I've had difficulty letting go."

"Difficulty?"

Silence.

"Looking back, certain incantations, certain premises, certain axioms were demonstrated to me...from these axioms followed conclusions that did not answer the questions...I was taught the rules at a young age. But then later, I was told that I was random matter...*chance*...that absolutes in terms of ethics were relative; the implications from this led to a sense of dread." Brief silence. "The inevitability of my dread was frustration, anger...self-pity... then disinterestedness. I became deeply cynical...and desperate for connection."

Silence.

"I see...and how old were you when you first started looking at pornography?"

Silence.

"I don't really remember...sometime after my parents' divorce...I was probably eleven or twelve when I found my father's videos."

"Would you say pornography was a habit of yours?"

Silence.

"I watched pornography, off and on, for many years...yes."

Silence.

"Off and on?"

"In my last year of college, I started dating. The experience was, for me, euphoric...I would go to church with her. For the most part I was indifferent to it. But eventually I became interested in the answers given to questions of value...meaning...absolutes."

Silence.

"I stopped watching porn during that time."

"I see. You sound disappointed?"

"I knew so little...about myself. I mean, I elevated my girlfriend...in my mind, I elevated her...she became my point of reference...an anchor. After college, I accepted a job as a business consultant...the work was interesting and went well for a couple of years, but I became dissatisfied. I ultimately accepted a position as chief fundraiser for a political party."

Silence.

"What was that like for you? Your professional life, I mean."

Silence.

"I suppose you could call it a catalytic experience...the political world can be...disorienting. Ethics, morality, and particular concepts tended to carry a utilitarian function—a means to an end. The ideals themselves were, for the most part, without content. They simply bred emotion...a feeling of uncertainty. What is certain is that my thoughts, especially at particular moments, were principally dissonant...almost schizophrenic, marked by contradictory feelings of apprehension and certainty, hesitation and faith, ambiguity and lucidity. The initial joy of knowing God became an exercise in fleetingness; it became a duty...I mistrusted God."

Silence.

"I see...why do you think you mistrusted God?"

"Partially from ignorance about his nature...and partially from sickness."

Silence.

"Sickness?"

Silence.

"Have you ever wondered about the nature of fear... the tendencies of disillusionment, bitterness, and cynicism? These states of being and the emotions related to them are not merely effects; they are, in turn, causes. I spent years consuming such trends...my mind could only handle so much...some kind of insanity was inevitable. I began to wonder if God could really meet me where I was...where I *am*...nothing really seems to change. I am sick of worrying all the time. The paranoia is extreme. I keep thinking in terms of punishment, rejection, ridicule, hypocrisy, and suicide. Somewhere along the line, I stopped caring. My relationship with God is disappointing. I hate him...my hate...I have realized that my life is nothing more than a kind of profanity...a kind of graffiti."

Silence.

"I see." Brief silence. "Thanks for calling into the show, Evan."